DELAYED INVASION

DELAYED INVASION

Claire Hollis, Ph.D.

Delayed Invasion

ISBN 0-9673122-3-x

Library of Congress Catalog Card Number: 99-96601

Printed in the United States of America

Published by   Warfare Publications
PMB#206
4577 Gunn Highway
Tampa, FL 33624 USA
(813) 265-2379
Fax: (813) 908-0228
E-mail: WarfareP@aol.com
Web site: www.warfareplus.com

Unless otherwise indicated, all scripture references are from the authorized *King James Version* of the Bible.

DELAYED INVASION

1

The day was overcast, it was misting rain, and things seemed just downright ugly as Reverend JJ Murphy and his wife drove into the city limits of Washington, D.C. Trash had accumulated on the sidewalks on both sides of the street from the downdrafts during the recent downpour, almost blocking the drainage gutters.

People hurried along with their heads bowed low, many looking unhappy and depressed. JJ and Lynn, his wife of thirty-seven years, watched the frowning pedestrians, clad in raincoats and holding their umbrellas in front of them like pieces of armor.

Puddles of water were everywhere, and cars splashed water on the people on the sidewalks and although it was only about noon, the sky was dark with clouds. The air was heavy with gloom and the wind often gusted, blowing at the pedestrians' umbrellas and swirling the trash about. It wasn't yet freezing, but the wind, coupled with the freezing rain, made the cold go all the way to the bone.

JJ and Lynn had been driving for several hours, greatly anticipating an appointment with a publisher who was interested in a book JJ had written. They had absolutely no inkling of the drama that was about to unfold right before their eyes.

Lynn had been napping for the past hour and JJ had made use of the time by popping an inspirational cassette into the player of their rental car. He had been wanting to listen to this one for months, but you know how it goes. His busy schedule of counseling, preparing sermons, teaching seminars, and the like, had not allowed it.

Just as the cassette clicked off, JJ glanced over at Lynn as she yawned and stretched herself back to consciousness, and he smiled. He felt so warm and secure being with her. He thought she was the most beautiful woman he had ever seen, both inside and out. Their marriage had been like a fairy tale because they were so perfectly suited for each other. Their relationship was harmonious and they were in agreement on most things. Disagreements rarely happened. In fact, they were so compatible that their friends and family were amazed.

As they stopped at a red light, happy to be close to their destination, Lynn casually glanced out the window. What she witnessed on the street in front of them made her shriek in terror! Startled, JJ looked out the window in the direction Lynn was pointing. Everything happened so quickly that they could hardly absorb it all.

Only thirty or forty feet away from their car, a very well-dressed and distinguished-looking man in his fifties with salt-and-pepper gray hair broke into a run. His face registered bewilderment and fear as two men brandishing handguns pursued him. They easily caught up to him and stuck their guns into his back.

JJ and Lynn were trying to understand what they were seeing when another element entered the drama. A black limousine pulled up to the curb and an elegantly dressed, tiny woman with shiny black hair, threw open the rear door. She jumped out and with unnatural strength, grabbed the man, and easily tossed him into the back seat. The victim hardly had time to resist, but JJ and Lynn could see him flailing his arms and thrashing about a bit. The two thugs jumped into the car, one in the back and one in the front, and the woman quickly closed the door on her side. The car sped away, leaving a wall of water on each side. This entire scene could not have taken more than twenty seconds. Maybe less. It was swift and otherworldly.

JJ and Lynn looked at each other in alarm, then JJ grabbed the cell phone and dialed 911.

"My wife and I just saw a man being forced into a limo and we think it was a kidnapping," he excitedly yelled at the emergency operator.

"Where are we? I don't even know. Let me look at the street sign." Glancing at the signpost on the corner, J.J. said, "Sir, we're at 14th Street and Eisenhower Boulevard."

JJ listened to the operator before replying, "Well, the man looked like he was in his fifties, and he had gray hair. He was just walking along the street, then he started to run when he saw two guys with guns. They caught up with him and forced him toward a limousine and there was a woman in the car that jumped out and threw him in. No, sir! We didn't notice the license number, but the limo was black and had a dent in the left rear fender. There was a bumper sticker that looked like a big black bird or something. Kinda like an eagle with a gold crown or crest of some sort on its head. Oh, by the way, they turned and headed west."

JJ gave the operator their cell phone number and told him that they could be contacted later in case they were needed. Then, with hands shaking slightly, he turned off the cell phone.

Lynn sighed loudly, "What a way to enter a city! If that was our welcoming committee, then I wonder what's next!"

"I think I can answer that question," JJ replied as he took a deep breath. "Did you get a close look at the woman in the limo?"

"No, I didn't pay much attention to her. I couldn't take my eyes off that poor man being kidnapped."

"Well, she sure looked like the woman named Lana that caused such an uproar at my nephew's church in Centerville. If it wasn't her, it must be her twin sister. Who would have thought she would still be in business after what happened to her there! I really wonder what she's doing here." JJ's voice was quizzical.

8

"Well, I guess there's nothing we can do now but just go on to the hotel. It would probably be more pleasant to stay on the outskirts of town, but I felt that the Holiday Inn in the middle of the city would be better because it might be a more convenient place for David to meet with me. Who would have thought that my childhood friend would become a big publisher? I can't wait for you to meet him." JJ actually sounded optimistic and expectant. However, he had no idea that they would soon become part of the drama they had witnessed.

As if to accentuate the turn the Murphys' day had taken, the rain began to beat down harder and the sky was turning darker as they drove into the heart of Washington, D.C. The wind even picked up dramatically, causing JJ to remark, "I think a tornado must be forming around here somewhere. It's getting so dark I can hardly see the street. It's been a long time since I've seen the rain come down in such torrents. Would you get out the map and help me with some directions, Honey?" he asked Lynn.

Lynn took the map out of the glove box and turned on the overhead light. The windshield wipers beat back and forth in a desperate attempt to clear the car's windshield. They squinted in an effort to see the street signs and about fifteen minutes later the Holiday Inn sign made them both feel more comfortable.

Because of the hideous weather, they splurged and let the hotel valet park their car. They quickly checked in to the hotel, dropped off their luggage in their room, and went downstairs to get some dinner. They were both famished, as they hadn't eaten since breakfast. They chose the quaint little cafe at the back of the hotel, instead of the elaborate dining room where most of the guests ended up.

After a juicy steak, baked potato, and hot apple pie *a la mode*, they settled down in their room. JJ flipped on the television, scarcely noticing what was being broadcast. He threw himself down into the large chair and Lynn began to unpack, reflecting on the events that had just unfolded in front of them.

Suddenly, the voice coming over the television commanded the attention of both JJ and Lynn. The newscaster was reporting and commenting on a kidnapping. Lynn sat down on the bed, almost frozen, and she and JJ stared at the picture of the man talking.

Timothy Blake, the famous network newscaster, appeared almost frantic as he spoke. "Michael Adams, Secretary of Defense, reportedly was kidnapped this afternoon. He slipped away from the Secret Service agent assigned to him and disappeared. We have a crew at his home and his wife, Carol, has agreed to give us some details of her husband's activities during the day." The remote TV camera switched to a close-up of Carol Adams.

Obviously trying to contain her anxiety, but maintaining her composure, Carol Adams responded to Timothy Blake. "Michael received a phone call this morning that clearly upset him. He acted strangely, very concerned, and when I asked him what was going on, he said he couldn't talk about it. He told me that he had to meet someone in private and that even though he wanted to, he couldn't tell me anything about it because it would put me and the children in danger. He did say, however, that it was of grave importance and that it was necessary for him to meet the person at a private location known to no one except him and the person he was meeting."

Timothy Blake started to ask a question, but refrained when he noticed Carol Adams subtly shake her head. He also saw that she was slightly trembling and he perceived, correctly, that she was terribly close to breaking down.

With his voice shaking, Timothy proceeded to read a short note that had been delivered to the *Washington Daily Herald*. **"We have Michael Adams!** That's all the note said! No ransom was mentioned, no threats—nothing!" Timothy Blake continued, "This station has received unconfirmed information that there was a witness to the kidnapping."

JJ and Lynn were transfixed as they listened, and looked at each other in absolute shock. JJ suddenly jumped up! He had forgotten that the 911 operator had told him to keep his cellular phone on. He grabbed for the cell phone that he had turned off earlier, and sure enough, as soon as he turned it on, he saw a message to call a local number.

JJ immediately dialed the number as Lynn sat motionless, her blue eyes opened wide. She was almost holding her breath in anticipation of what was coming next. It seemed like JJ's fingers wouldn't cooperate as he tried to dial the number. What a contrast for hands that were so coordinated that he had been on championship basketball teams in high school and college. These were fingers that could easily type 55-60 words a minute when writing sermons or manuscripts.

JJ tried dialing the number again, and his voice was quivering as he said, "Yes, sir! I'm the man that called 911. Yes, I reported the kidnapping. Where am I now? Well, my wife and I are at the downtown Holiday Inn in Room 113. You're gonna do *what*? OK! We'll be ready."

JJ's hands were shaking as he put down the phone.

"Lynn, that was the FBI and someone will be here to pick us up in ten minutes. This is unbelievable! They are going to take us directly to the White House to speak with the President. The President! Can you believe this? What we saw this afternoon has something to do with national security."

"Did the man give you any details?"

"No, Honey; he just said that what we saw was the kidnapping of Secretary of Defense Adams." JJ said hesitantly. "Can you believe this? All I wanted to do is get my book published. My appointment tomorrow with David is at two o'clock and I hope all this doesn't interfere. I know this book is inspired by God Himself, and right now getting it published is a top priority in my life."

Catching his breath, JJ conveyed a sense of urgency to Lynn that caught her attention. His demeanor was very serious and Lynn began to grasp the gravity of their situation just by observing her husband.

JJ grabbed Lynn's hand and she knew they were going to pray—it was customary for them to hold hands when they prayed. "Lynn, let's pray before they get here." Humbly, JJ prayed with great strength, "Dear heavenly Father, You know what's going on, and we don't. We ask You to send your angels around us as we go to see the President. Please, dear Lord, give us total recall and clarity of mind that we can be of some benefit and…"

Before JJ could get out another word, there was a banging on the door. When he opened it, he and Lynn were both surprised to see four big men in dark suits and khaki raincoats standing in the hallway. All but one of the men had a hand tucked inside his suit coat and it was easy to assume that there were guns in those hands. JJ said a quick prayer that conveyed his fear, "Please, God, *let these guys be FBI agents.*"

JJ glanced back at Lynn and their eyes met with a puzzled look as if to say, "What on earth is going on here?"

The apparent leader of the four men flashed his credentials, which, indeed, identified him as an FBI agent. The other three men quickly searched around the room and the bath. As he picked up JJ's cell phone from the bed and placed it in his raincoat pocket, the man in charge motioned for one of the other men to check outside the window. Then two of them went out and stationed themselves at each end of the hallway.

The agents in the room took JJ and Lynn by the arm as the man in charge said, "Please get your purse, Madam, and both of you put on your coats. Your belongings will be moved to a safer place tonight. We'll pick up your car on the way out."

JJ and Lynn were rather overwhelmed with the whole procedure, especially when the lead man became rather officious. "Come on, now…let's go!"

His voice was stern and abrupt, and the Murphys were rapidly escorted out of the room in which they had yet to spend the night. So much for settling in for the evening!

JJ and Lynn clutched each other's hands tightly as they were swiftly whisked down the hall to the back stairs. Descending the stairs almost two at a time, they saw yet another man in a khaki raincoat holding the door open to the outside.

A vehicle was waiting with its motor running and a man with an umbrella took JJ by the arm. JJ continued to cling tightly to Lynn, and the two found themselves being placed in the back seat of the car.

As they got situated in their seat, the man in charge jumped in beside them. His attitude became solicitous as he said almost apologetically, "I'm so sorry about all this. You must be wondering what in the world is going on. I can only tell you that what you two witnessed today is of extreme importance to our national security. In fact, to *world* security!"

The car phone rang and the man in charge picked it up. "Yes, sir, Mr. President. We have them, and we're on our way. We'll be at the White House in twenty minutes."

Lynn and JJ were almost in shock and they just sat silently staring into space. What could all this mean? National security? The White House? The President of the United States? What on earth is going on here? They could almost read each other's minds.

They drove up to the security gate and were waved right on through. Within minutes JJ and Lynn were shaking hands with President Peter

Roland in some anteroom of the West Wing of 1600 Pennsylvania Avenue.

After the usual introductions, the President spoke. "Please be seated," he said, as he attempted to make the Murphys comfortable in an uncomfortable situation. "Would you like something hot to drink? Coffee, tea, hot chocolate?"

Moving quickly to the unpleasant matters at hand, and looking squarely at JJ, President Roland said "I want you to tell me everything you saw today. We need every detail. I can't adequately impress on you how very important this is, so please take your time."

JJ began, "Yes, sir. Well, first, Mr. President, I think we could use some hot chocolate to help us calm down. The past half hour has been rather baffling and alarming, to say the least." The President nodded, as if sympathizing with the Murphys, and one of the FBI agents left the room, presumably to get their drinks.

JJ started to relate the kidnapping event. "It was somewhere around noon, and we were just coming into the city. We were stopped at a light when my wife glanced out the window. She saw what was happening and screamed, so then I looked and watched it all happen, as well."

Turning to Lynn, the President said, "Please tell me exactly what you saw."

Lynn was nearly overwhelmed by all of this and was holding tightly to JJ's hands. Trying to remain calm and collected, she slowly began to tell the President and the others what she and her husband had seen.

"A man was walking down the street and then he suddenly started running. I saw two men with guns in their hands chasing him and when they caught him, they jammed their guns in his back. A black limousine pulled up to the curb and a petite woman held the rear door open. The men pushed the gentleman toward the car and the woman got out into the street area, reached over, and grabbed the man. She threw him into the back of the limo as the two gunmen got in the car. She seemed *really* strong for her size! I remember thinking she must be a relative of Wonder Woman to have strength like that! The limo took off at a tremendous speed, spraying water on both sides of their car." Lynn looked at JJ as he nodded in agreement.

Resting his chin on his forefinger, the President replied, "Would you recognize the two men or the woman?"

"I personally wouldn't recognize any of them, but my husband got a good look at the woman as she got out of the car to grab the man," Lynn said as she thanked the FBI agent who handed her a cup of hot chocolate. He handed a second cup to JJ.

The President picked up a photo off of his desk and handed it to Mrs. Murphy. "Is this the man who was kidnapped?"

"Yes, sir, it is! I recognized him from the picture on the newscast we were watching at the hotel. It's Michael Adams."

At that point JJ spoke up. "Mr. President, the tiny woman had coal black hair pulled back into a bun. She was extremely well dressed; her long black coat had black fur around the collar and cuffs. One thing about her caught my attention and stayed in my mind. Her lipstick was extremely noticeable—very, very bright red. She wore earrings that sparkled like clusters of diamonds, and black leather boots with high heels. She bore a striking resemblance to a woman I saw recently while visiting my nephew," JJ said and took a sip of his hot chocolate.

The President asked, "Would you recognize her if you saw her again?"

"I believe so, sir."

"I want to know all the details. I have the 911 report, so I know the time and location, but describe the limo for me. Did you see the driver?"

"No sir," JJ replied, "I didn't see the driver, but I did see that he was wearing a chauffeur's hat. The limo was black and had a noticeable dent in the left rear fender. A bumper sticker had a logo or symbol on it that looked like a bird, maybe an eagle with a gold crown on its head. I was looking at that bumper sticker and didn't notice the license plate number. Sorry, sir. Anyway, the limo made a left turn at the next stoplight."

The President continued politely grilling the two for information. "Were there other cars or pedestrians who might have witnessed this, as well?"

JJ spoke up. "There were people on the sidewalks, but they all seemed to have their heads lowered, trying to escape the cold wind and rain. We were the only ones sitting at the stoplight, and there were no cars passing in front of us. I'm sure we were the only car around at that moment. The whole thing happened in seconds. The limo seemed to come out of nowhere—maybe there was an alley there, I don't know! It all happened on the side of the street closest to us. The limo pulled over to the men, Michael Adams was thrown in, and then they took off so quickly. It was quick as a flash!"

"What do you remember about the two gunmen?" queried President Roland.

"Everything they had on was black," JJ responded, quite sure of what he had seen. As the President looked over at her, Lynn nodded in agreement and took another drink of her hot chocolate.

JJ went on with his description. "Black shoes, black pants, black trench coats. One man was blond and the other had dark hair. I only got a glimpse of their faces because they were moving too fast and the rain made it hard to see. I'm sure I couldn't recognize them again, but I did notice what could have been a scar across the face of the blond man, whose hair was quite long. The guy with the dark hair had his cut really short, close to a buzzcut. They were about the same height, probably six feet or so." JJ sipped his hot chocolate and continued, "I remember the woman seemed very tiny as she stood near them."

"What happened to the two men?"

"They jumped into the limo while the woman was still tossing Michael Adams into the back. Right, Honey?" he said, as he glanced at his wife. She nodded.

Then there was complete silence as Lynn and JJ each took another sip from their cups. They were edgy and unsure of all that was going on. Slowly, however, the realization of where they were and with whom they were speaking began to sink in.

They looked around the room and noticed that everyone's face had a frown on it. The room was charged with the feeling of impending danger, anxiety, frustration and deep concern. Minutes passed before the President's voice broke the silence.

"I'm sorry, but we have to move you to a more secure place. I know this is terribly unsettling for you, but you will be totally protected. Our guards will be with you twenty-four hours a day. However, for your own safety, you will not be able to make any phone calls or contact anyone at all until we release you." The President's voice was kind but firm.

"Your lives are in grave danger. The 911 report has leaked out to the media and your cell phone number will be traced in order to find out who you are. They can obtain a report as quickly as we did. They can get your names, address, occupation, family and medical information, social security numbers, and tax information. Reverend Murphy, the media can really be a nuisance sometimes." He had noticed the surprised look on JJ's face.

"We consider this situation a national security threat and are keeping the media in check. At present, they cannot move on any information regarding you two, but the threat to your lives is very real. We must keep you in a safe place. I deeply apologize for any inconvenience, but we have no choice. The Secretary is in even more imminent danger than either of you."

Changing the subject for the first time, President Roland asked JJ, "By the way, Reverend Murphy, our data indicates that you are a preacher, but there is no denomination listed in our information. What church are you associated with?"

JJ spoke up, "I'm an evangelist, sir. I speak in many churches of all denominations."

JJ then took a deep breath and asked, "Mr. President, may I say a few words?"

"Yes, of course, Reverend Murphy, by all means."

"My wife and I came to Washington on business. I have recently written a book, and I had made an appointment at two o'clock tomorrow with an old buddy who is a successful publisher. It's very important that I meet with him. Would that be a problem?"

"Reverend Murphy, you have no idea what you're asking. You and your wife are the only ones who can help us with this urgent problem. Believe me, sir, this situation is not only our problem, but yours, as well. And everyone who lives on this planet."

"What kind of book have you written?" inquired President Roland, almost as an afterthought.

JJ replied, "Well, sir, it's all about exposing the enemy and how to expel him from your life."

"The enemy? And what enemy would that be, Reverend?"

"Why, Satan and his kingdom," JJ replied, with a serious expression on his face.

The President smiled and glanced at the other men in the room, who seemed to chuckle under their breath and pass a cynical look from one to the other. Lynn thought to herself, "It's bad enough that the average person doesn't really believe in the power of the evil one, let alone the leader of the free world."

"Reverend Murphy, right now the devil is the least of our worries. We have a problem in the real world that has the potential of annihilating this entire planet. And you have landed right in the middle of it!" President Roland crossed his arms, leaned toward JJ, and gave him a stern look.

The President's expression softened as he continued, "Tell you what we'll do. If you will go along with our program and not contact anyone, I'll make sure that your book gets published when this thing is over. I read at least one book a week, so give me your manuscript, and I'll read through it myself."

Returning to the matter at hand, President Roland then said, "My men will take you to a safe place now. But if you remember anything else about what you saw this afternoon, no matter how minor you think it may be, please call me. A line will be set up so that you can reach me direct at any time." With that, the President stood up, shook hands with both JJ and Lynn, and watched as they were escorted from the room.

Claire Hollis, Ph.D.

DELAYED INVASION

2

J and Lynn walked down a windowless hallway and out onto the White House lawn where a helicopter waited for them. Accompanied by three FBI agents, they joined the crew of two who were seated behind the controls in the front cabin. After about a thirty-minute flight, the helicopter landed in what looked like an open field on a farm. It was now dark outside, but lights flashed intermittently to show the copter where to land. A car was waiting near the landing area, and they all were out of there as fast as they had come in.

JJ and Lynn felt helpless as they were being driven in the night to some unknown destination. They looked at each other frequently and silently prayed for protection and wisdom.

After about fifteen minutes, the car slowed almost to a stop and the driver turned out the vehicle lights. The storm had pretty much moved out of the region, so the full moon provided a small amount of light. JJ and Lynn could see no houses or any type of structure around. However, they could see a hill or mound of some sort directly in front of them and the car slowly advanced toward it. Why were they driving into that hill?

Slowly the "hill" opened up and the car proceeded forward, as if it were going into a garage. As soon as the mound that formed the door was closed, lights came on, illuminating a narrow tunnel. Slowly the car advanced through the tunnel and came out in a parking area big enough to accommodate several cars. Dim lighting emanated from lamps hanging on the walls. Two nondescript doors were spaced evenly apart at the end of the parking area and the driver eased the car near one of the doors and parked.

"Well," one of the FBI agents said, breaking the silence, "we're home! Let's go inside."

JJ and Lynn knew they were being "instructed" to get out of the car and follow the men through the door. An agent popped the trunk open and removed their baggage.

Seeing the questioning looks on the faces of JJ and Lynn, the agent said, "Your personal belongings will be with you at all times and you will get your rental car back later." Lynn, the one who wrote the checks in the family, wondered who was going to pay the extra fee to the rental car company. She wisely concluded that this was no time for questions, even pragmatic ones.

They entered an elegant, tasteful reception area furnished with rich, mahogany furniture, original paintings, well-maintained plants, large, ornate mirrors, and expensive carpets. The most dramatic furnishing, however, was the framed Presidential Seal hanging on the wall behind the desk. Heavy, brass lamps provided subdued lighting, creating an almost ethereal atmosphere. Two more federal agents appeared, greeted them, then discreetly disappeared.

One of the agents accompanying them finally introduced himself as Paul and said politely, "Reverend Murphy, Mrs. Murphy, if you will follow me, I'll take you to your quarters. You'll find your stay here pleasant, I hope. Your accommodations are equal to any four-star hotel in the world." He opened a sliding glass door hidden in a mirrored wall and led them to their rooms. The other agents stayed behind to tend to some paperwork in the reception area.

When JJ and Lynn saw their suite, they could hardly believer their eyes. They looked at each other and JJ said, "This sure isn't like anything we are accustomed to."

JJ and Lynn had noticed several other people when they entered this "building" and JJ took this opportunity to ask Paul who they were.

"Those are security agents who are here to not only protect you, but to accommodate you and make you comfortable. Don't hesitate to let them know if you have any needs whatsoever."

Pausing, Paul continued, "Reverend Murphy, if you'll please give me the manuscript, I'll make sure the President receives it later tonight."

Their luggage had not been brought into their room yet, and JJ couldn't help having the suspicion that it was being searched.

As Paul showed Lynn and JJ the suite and explained the nature of the compound in which they were being housed, an agent entered with their bags, smiled, and quietly left the room. JJ opened a suitcase and handed his prized manuscript to Paul.

"Folks, if you would like to eat or drink, just pick up the white telephone and request it. If you need to speak with the President, pick up the red phone. We are at your disposal and want you to be comfortable. You will find all kinds and sizes of pillows, blankets and towels in the closets. There is a steam room and an exercise room off the bathroom. Have a good night's rest and know that you are totally secure and protected here." With that, Paul excused himself courteously, and with JJ's manuscript in hand, left the room.

JJ and Lynn just stood looking at each other.

"Lynn, I don't know what this is all about, but let's just consider it the blessing of God and enjoy it. I've never even seen a place this opulent in my entire life," he said, looking around the room and walking over to the entertainment center just a few steps away. "It's straight out of a James Bond movie! Except for the absence of windows, you'd never guess that we're underground. This place is fit for a king!"

"Or a president, Dear. I certainly agree. Let's order a snack, then get cleaned up. I wonder what's on the menu," she said, picking up the leather-bound menu on the table by the couch. After a short discussion with JJ, she ordered their snack.

There were "His" and "Hers" bathrooms, which were loaded with an elaborate assortment of bath oils, perfumes, soaps, hair products, cosmetics, towels and robes. Everything for their comfort—total luxury.

After refreshing showers, they emerged from their bathrooms almost simultaneously and glanced over at the huge bed with the tapestry canopy. The spread had been pulled back and by the expression on their faces, they knew each other's thoughts: We really have absolutely no privacy here!

"Our snack should be ready by now," Lynn remarked. In less than a minute, a light knock on the door signaled the arrival of a server, who announced that their snack was ready in their private dining room. *Their private dining room!*

As JJ and Lynn ate the delicious snack, they shared their thoughts about the day's events and tried to keep their deep concern, bordering on fear, under control.

They were exhausted, both physically and emotionally, and needed rest. As was their custom, they knelt down together before retiring, and JJ led in prayer.

"Heavenly Father, *we* know that *You* know exactly what is going on. We acknowledge that You guide and direct our lives and that we're not here by mistake. We just want to make sure that we stay in a position that we can be of service to You. Help us not to fear and forgive us if we've done anything today that displeases you in any way.

"Cover us with the blood of your Son, Jesus, and fill us with the power of your Holy Spirit. Let us be dressed in the full armor of God, and put a guard across our mouths so that we will say only what You want to say through us. We drive out any evil force that may be in this room. We ask You, dear heavenly Father, to dispatch your almighty warring angels to encamp around this place and hold back the forces of Satan and his kingdom while we sleep.

"Give us a good night's rest. We speak peace into the situation surrounding the President and this kidnapping. We pray for the safety of Michael Adams and his loved ones. In Jesus' Name we pray, amen."

Getting into bed, the tired couple were mildly amused, but not exactly surprised, to see the lights go off automatically. This time, however, one of them voiced the feeling they had had earlier: "Yeah, we really are being taken care of—maybe a little *too well*!" No privacy at all.

DELAYED INVASION

3

The woman named Lana was screaming, "Yoooou idiots! Can't you ever do anything right? Do I have to do everything myself? I told you to keep him awake all night with a light shining in his eyes and the tape playing. Why did you let him sleep? You've ruined my whole day!"

Keeping her eyes on the captive, Michael Adams, Lana lined up the four men in a row and stared intently at them. As she focused her dark eyes on them, they were all "zapped" as though struck by lightning, and suddenly "flew" up onto the wall midway between the ceiling and the floor. They were pinned in place as if glued there by the very force of evil itself.

After Lana screeched and reprimanded each one, she forcefully told them to get out of her sight, and they disappeared through the wall.

Michael Adams could not believe what he had just witnessed. He sat terrified, wondering what was going to happen next. He silently begged her to stay away from him! Futile wish, however.

The mysterious female quickly swung around and pointed her bony finger at Michael. If he had not believed in evil incarnate before, this woman was quickly changing his mind. She held some sort of power that he could feel from ten feet away. How could she pin those men up against the wall like that with just a look? Who was this woman? Her long red nails matched the red lipstick and the red dress she was wearing. Her coal black hair and diamond earrings were glistening in the single ray of the morning sunlight seeping in through a crack that was visible by the window that was covered with a black cloth.

"Soooooooo, Michael Adams! That military crew that you had stationed in Germany wasn't only able to break the codes of these earth people who are your enemies, but they somehow stumbled into the supernatural realm and were able to track us down and eavesdrop on us, too. Mankind is getting a little too smart for itself, and that's why we have planned our takeover." Her voice reminded Michael of what he thought witches sounded like when he was a boy.

"You see, Michael Adams, our leader is the prince of the power of the air. The minute your crew contacted you with our coded information, we immediately set you up for the kidnapping. I know that you got to the President with the message that the earth will be taken over on the thirteenth, but I also know that is *all* he knows. He thinks the earth will be destroyed, but all we're going to do is take it over," she sneered, leaning down to stare into his face.

Michael sat straight up when she mentioned his crew. He wondered if they were safe.

As if reading Michael's mind, Lana cackled, "All five crew members have been eliminated. Even though you told them to run and hide, and they made a great effort, we found them. Nothing gets by us. We have comrades everywhere; some are visible, some are not. We know everything that's going on at all times, everywhere," laughed the mysterious woman in red. She looked so wicked! Michael shuddered at the sight (and sound) of her.

"Michael Adams, you're a dead man. The only reason I am keeping you alive is to toy with the President and play around with the world. My comrades take great joy in seeing humans squirm in fear," she said, gloating.

"When we invade the earth on the thirteenth, everyone will think that we came from outer space. Our leader wants to be recognized as the leader of the entire earth. He wants to be worshipped by everyone of you, and have all you silly little humans bow down to him. Our people are busy setting up his headquarters at this very moment."

Michael still did not respond and showed very little emotion. That further angered Lana.

"What can you do, Michael Adams? You're a powerful man! You are in a powerful country." She taunted him mercilessly.

"*Nothing*! That's what you can do—*absolutely nothing*! It's out of your hands. It's out of everyone's hands. We will rule! The fact is, we rule the earth right now, but hardly anyone is aware of it. We want to 'come out of the closet' and be recognized for all our accomplishments and deeds. We deserve it!"

With no warning, the room was full of people. Lana turned around, glared at them, and blurted out, "Throw this pitiful man in the back room and guard him until I return."

Michael Adams was by no means a "pitiful" man. He was a kind-looking man with graying hair and compassionate blue eyes. Short in stature and highly intelligent, he had graduated from the military academy with highest honors. He was a man of integrity and had been handpicked by the President not only because of his experience and intelligence, but also because he was trustworthy.

Michael's father had been a pioneer pastor, building churches and giving himself totally to the spreading of the gospel of Jesus Christ. Michael Adams knew a lot about the Bible, God and the devil, but he be had been very hurt during his teenage years and rebelled against the teaching of his father. He loved and respected his mother and father, but he made a decision not to follow their life of faith.

Michael's wife, Carol, came from a long line of aristocrats who were social climbers, primarily interested in money, position and recognition. Sadly, their two children followed in their mother's footsteps and were spoiled rich kids.

At the bidding of the woman in red, the Secretary of Defense was hurled into a completely empty, dirty, dark room. After Lana's minions left, Michael walked over to a corner, stood with his back to the wall, then slipped slowly to the floor, almost like butter melting. He sank onto the floor, his head in his hands, and tears began to stream down his face.

Fear was foreign to Michael Adams, but two realizations made his heart pound and his breath come in short gasps. Could it possibly be that he would never see his family again? Was the world really about to be invaded by demonic entities? He shook his head in disbelief as he began to mutter to himself.

"I address you, God. I am speaking to the God that my parents served. If You are real, show yourself to me now."

Michael realized he was *praying*! Praying to a God he had firmly declared he did not believe existed. At that moment he realized that all these years he had lived a lie and his nonchalant, worldly facade had masked a yearning in the core of his being that he now recognized as a hunger to know God, the God of his father!

Realizing this truth made Michael feel hypocritical because he felt he was only praying because he was in desperate need. "What a jerk I am! What a jerk I've been all these years! Well, all God can do is ignore me, and I can understand if He does. So here goes nothing!"

Michael began to pray some more, this time with a small element of faith involved, more confidence filling his heart. Then he felt a comfortable warmth spread over him and he sensed that God *maybe* had heard his prayer. Even though his eyes were closed, he could see a great light, a light so bright that when he opened his eyes, it almost blinded him. He was so shocked that he feared the demon woman (he didn't realize how accurate this characterization was) or one of her henchmen was shining a bright flashlight of some sort in his face. But no, he was still alone. Unbelievably, the light came straight out of *nowhere* and it made him feel safe. "It must be coming from heaven," Michael thought to himself. "Yes, implausible as it seems, the light is from heaven!"

"Oh, God, YOU ARE REAL!" He closed his eyes again and this time he knew he was talking to a loving Father who was listening to him.

"Please, Father, I have lived my life without You and I have ignored You. I have even joked about You and used your Name in vain. I have sinned, Father, but please forgive me. I always thought somewhere in the back of my mind that your Son, Jesus, was real and that He really did die for all my sins. Today I acknowledge it as truth, and I believe it and I give what's left of my life to You right now."

Michael felt fear give way to peace and when he finished his prayer, the beam of light disappeared into his chest.

Michael thought he saw something move in the corner of the room and turning in that direction, he saw an extremely tall man standing quietly. He rubbed his eyes. Was he hallucinating? Had the "light" been a hallucination, as well? Did the man across the room shine a bright light at him and blind him? Michael was suddenly confused. Was he imagining things that were not really occurring? Michael thought he might be losing his mind, and he cried out to God again, "Dear God, what's happening to me?"

Michael opened his eyes again and looked across the room. Yes, the "apparition" was still there, very tall and very real. Was he an angel?

Michael judged the ceiling of the room to be about twenty feet high, and the man stood at least ten feet tall. He held a sword in his hand and as he motioned for Michael to come to him, he smiled. Was he really there? Well, perhaps not physically, but he was definitely a presence from God. Michael's jaw dropped open as he stared at this marvelous angelic being.

Michael knew the man was real, in one realm or another, so he decided to obey him. Now, instead of fear, Michael felt increasing peace. Love began to flow through every fiber of his being as he slowly got off the floor and walked toward the being. The tall man pointed to a board in the wall and motioned for Michael to go over to it.

Although the room was so dark he could barely see, Michael went to the board and pulled at it. He managed to loosen the board just enough to get his hand inside, and he touched what felt like a book. He was able to maneuver the object out of the hole and saw that, indeed, it was a book, and that it was grimy with cobwebs and dust. As he was blowing off the dust, he reached out to show the book to the man, but he had disappeared into thin air! Michael was having a hard time comprehending all that was happening but strangely, he felt calm and peaceful. He knew he was not alone. And he was no longer afraid—of anything or anyone.

Michael could barely make out the two words on the book: HOLY BIBLE. He opened it and could scarcely believe what he read handwritten on the flyleaf (in very large letters):

I am a carpenter
Working on this building.
I am placing this Bible within these walls
Because the God I serve
Is impressing on me
That one day it will be found,
And the person who finds it
Will need it as desperately
As the air we breathe.
God bless you,
And may it mean as much to you
As it means to me.

Michael cradled the Word of God in his arms...and wept tears of joy—mixed with regret.

DELAYED INVASION

4

JJ and Lynn awoke about the same time, looked around the grand room they had slept in, and tried to fully comprehend the events that had put them in this situation. Had it all been a dream? Apparently not, because here they were, lying in a bed fit for a king. They clasped hands and JJ began to pray, another custom they had—prayer first thing in the morning. JJ had scarcely said "amen" when the white phone by the bed rang.

"What would you like for breakfast?" the professional voice at the other end of the line inquired.

"Hold on a minute, please. Wow, Lynn, they want to take our order for breakfast. Can you believe this?"

"Well, I can believe almost anything now, but I'm still puzzled at how they know exactly what's going on in this room—even the moment we wake up and finish praying. This is getting a little weird, don't you think?"

"I agree with you, Honey. But they're waiting for our order."

"Okay, go ahead and order for us. Anything will do for me."

Struggling to gain his composure, JJ ordered ham with scrambled eggs, toasted English muffins, fresh fruit and decaffeinated coffee.

"Coming right up, sir. Feel free to come out in your robes—and use the robes provided for you, if you haven't already. Breakfast will be on the table in your dining room in ten minutes."

When JJ told Lynn that breakfast would be served in ten minutes "in our private dining room," she smiled her approval, giggled, and remarked, "Sure beats eating at home, doesn't it?" They were so carried away with everything that momentarily they forgot the seriousness of their situation. They jumped out of bed and playfully joked around as they freshened up, anticipating their "servant" waiting on them.

Breakfast was on time, beautifully presented, and eagerly devoured. JJ and Lynn kept their conversation light, but they were already beginning to come back to earth and sense the gravity of what was going on.

They were just getting started with their unpacking in preparation for the day when the red telephone rang.

"This is totally unbelievable!" JJ looked at Lynn and shook his head in disbelief. "Imagine the President of the United States personally calling us."

JJ picked up the phone. "Good morning!"

"Good morning, Reverend Murphy. I hope you slept well."

"Yes, sir, we did, thank you."

The President continued, "I have been thinking about something you said last night. You mentioned that the woman you saw reminded you of someone you had seen before. Who is that person? Where does she live? What do you know about her?"

JJ gulped. "The lady's name is Lana. We saw her in Centerville, the town where my nephew lives. We were there about a week ago and this lady was causing a lot of trouble. She had a group of people, thirteen in all, I believe, and she was the leader. She seemed to control all these other people."

JJ paused for a moment, trying desperately to remember any details that might be important.

"We were told that she and her group flew into Centerville once a month to conduct meetings with three prominent townspeople: the mayor, the banker and a preacher. She seemed to exercise control over them, as well, and the rumor around town was that she was into occult activities. I overheard one of the men, I think it was the banker, say that he saw her actually change her appearance right before his eyes."

The President broke in and asked, "Excuse me, Reverend, but did you say she changed her appearance? Her physical appearance?"

"That's what he said, Mr. President. He said she would puff up and become so big that she almost filled the room she was in. I couldn't really fathom it when he told me, but he swore it was true. Even though I don't have too much firsthand knowledge, I can refer you to some of the others that were involved. Any one of the three I mentioned could tell you a lot more than I can."

After motioning to Lynn to hand him his address book, JJ continued, "My nephew's name is Pastor Terry Murphy and his phone number is 222-555-6066. He would be able to give you information on any of the others involved."

JJ listened for a moment more. "Oh, yes, Mr. President, we're very comfortable. If we can be of any other help to you, just let us know." JJ hung up the phone and looked at Lynn's puzzled face.

"JJ, are you sure that the woman we saw yesterday was the same one who came to Centerville and caused all that trouble?"

"Well, Lynn, I don't know for certain, but you can be assured that if she is, the government will find out, and it won't take them very long."

JJ was quiet for a moment, a pensive expression on his face. Then he said quietly, "Since we have to stay in this place all day, let's make it productive. We need to spend the day in prayer. Agreed?"

"Absolutely! There's evidently a state of emergency and if this country is in trouble, we need to call on God to intervene. And we need to bind up the powers of Satan and his kingdom, because he obviously is up to something big."

Claire Hollis, Ph.D.

DELAYED INVASION

5

The entire White House was in an uproar. Important people kept coming and going all night long and the staff knew that something dreadful was happening. Everyone seemed to be frowning and a feeling of gloom and foreboding permeated the atmosphere.

The President had called in his cabinet members and other heads of government. Sometimes several people would go in together, and at other times someone would go in alone. But no matter who went in, they all left in a hurry, all with a frown.

While no one knew for sure what went on behind those closed doors, it later became clear that they had all received the same report. What report? The report of impending danger, even disaster! A threat of a world invasion on the thirteenth.

The mandate was clear: Do not let the public know what is going on. We cannot afford panic, but get your people prepared. Put the military on alert! Do whatever is necessary in your jurisdiction to be ready for anything.

Before calling in these important leaders, President Roland had called several heads of state around the world and not one of them knew anything about any threats, let alone an invasion of the world. Still, he had to go ahead on the strength of what he had heard through his intelligence sources.

In the Oval Office, the President swiveled his chair around and stared out his window into the grand, well-manicured gardens surrounding the White House. His expression was stern and stoic, yet he was frustrated and extremely concerned. His advisors had been of some help, but he knew that he was the ultimate authority, and that knowledge weighed heavily on him.

His staff was allowing him time to be alone, and as he concentrated on the gravity of the present situation, he became almost trancelike. It sure would feel good just to drift away and land on some idyllic island where he could put all this behind him. How he needed peace!

President Roland was startled out of his reverie by the ringing of the phone.

"Find him! Use everyone and every source available to find Michael Adams. This is imperative! Michael is the only one who really knows what's going on!" The President's voice was angry and loud.

"I know all about that, but you must declare this mission a priority. This could affect the entire world! And you know the media is having a heyday with Michael's kidnapping."

The President listened for a couple of minutes, then said, more calmly, "Well, Michael is the central figure in this whole debacle because he has top secret info. Information we need! I know you're doing your best—but like I said, you have my authorization to use every possible available avenue to get to the bottom of this. Report back to me every hour with your progress. Surely it can't be that hard to find a black limousine with a big dent in the fender and a flashy bumper sticker."

President Roland slammed down the receiver and just at that moment, Director Campbell of the Secret Service came through the door. He was slightly out of breath and before he could say a word, the President asked, "What have you found out about the black eagle with the gold crown?"

"Mr. President, you're probably not going to believe this, but the eagle with the crown is a symbol used in the occult. There is a highly secret group of people who worship Satan and they use this symbol to notify others that they are part of the group."

"Do you know the name of the group?"

"Not yet, Mr. President, but we did find out that they sometimes have the symbol tattooed on obvious parts of their body for the same reason. Identification. We haven't even been able to find information about the leaders of the group. I have heard there are a total of thirteen leaders and that they meet secretly once a month. So, as you can see, it's all very covert. Apparently they have infiltrated city and state governments, schools, and even the upper echelons of major corporations."

The President interrupted, "Do you know any of the corporations they're in?"

"Strange as it may seem, Mr. President, our intelligence has been unable to come up with anything there, either. We can't even find where they meet; we got close, but for obvious reasons, they have started to move around. One more thing that makes this difficult is that we really can't find any wrongdoing. After all, this is their religion, and they certainly have freedom to practice *that*."

"Wait just a minute! Did you say these people worship Satan? Well, for the first time since it began, this thing is beginning to make a little sense to me". He pushed the intercom on his phone. "Cindy, please get me the mayor of Centerville!" He waited while she rang the number.

"Director, please wait while I talk to the Mayor of Centerville."

DELAYED INVASION

6

It was a slow day in the small town of Centerville and Mayor Casey propped his feet on his desk, leaned back in his oversized leather chair, and took a snooze. Official papers, phone messages, candy wrappers and assorted clutter obliterated the top of his expensive desk. The thick layer of dust on his furniture was at least six months old, and when the light was just right, one could even see the dust hovering in the air.

Centerville had won awards for its immaculate landscaping and picture perfect buildings, but the mayor's private office was a different story. And his personal appearance didn't do much to help the situation. Grossly overweight, his belly hung over his belt, and nothing he did improved his appearance, because he was just *sloppy*. That's the only word to describe him. His mouth was partially open as he napped and his thick black mustache wiggled as he snored. His secretary entered his office only when she was summoned because she always had the urge to dust and vacuum. And she was allergic to dust!

The shrill ringing of the phone jolted Mayor Casey awake and he almost fell off his chair.

"Hello. Mayor Casey here," he said as authoritatively as possible, trying to sound awake.

"Who? Oh, yeah, *right*! If you're the President, I'm Superman. Now who is this and what do you want? I have important work to do." Actually, he was only half-awake and he wanted to finish his nap.

"Mayor Casey, I assure you this is President Roland. I want you to tell me everything you can about a woman named Lana and the group she belongs to. We have reason to believe that she and her cohorts have been holding secret, late-night meetings in your town."

Mayor Casey recognized the President's voice and sputtered, "Mr. President, sir, I'm sorry! Please forgive me! And believe me, I am not a part of that group anymore." Mayor Casey stopped and thought, "I've already said too much! Boy, am I in trouble now. Stay calm—stay cool."

"Mr. President, sir, Lana and her group scared the dickens out of everybody in town. I swear, Mr. President, that woman had powers that were not even human. She was, like, supernatural and she forced us to do what she wanted. I know that makes us sound weak, but we were scared of her because she demonstrated power that was not human. It was supernatural, I swear."

"Are you saying, Mayor Casey, that this woman might have had something to do with Satan?"

"Oh, definitely, definitely! Although it took us a while to pick up on that aspect of it. These people came to town and held their meetings, and even forced some of us to attend, as I mentioned."

"What made you figure out that they were up to no good?" asked President Roland.

"Well, things went along smoothly until Pastor Terry's uncle and his wife came to visit. It seemed like their presence drove Lana and the rest of them out of town forever. I never really understood all of it, but there were rumors that they were filled with some kind of light, something from Jesus and God. Later, most of us in the town found out about it firsthand." Mayor Casey started to elaborate, but the President interrupted him.

"Mayor Casey, you've been most helpful and I appreciate your time." The mayor began to feel relieved. "But I do have several more questions. What are the names of Pastor Murphy's aunt and uncle?"

"The uncle's name is JJ Murphy and his wife's name is Lynn. Very fine people, I assure you. Lana and her group never gave any last names; at least if they did, I never heard them. They let me and two other town leaders sit in on their meetings while they discussed Centerville, but before we knew what was happening, she started ordering *us* around. And after she gave us our orders, we had to leave so they could talk confidentially. Their meetings would go through the night and we would take them back to the airport outside of town where they kept a private plane."

"What else can you tell me?"

The mayor was starting to get anxious again, even fearful. What was going on here?

"Well, like I said, sir, Lana could do supernatural things and she had incredible strength. It was really weird, because she was such a small little gal. Sometime I thought even her strength was supernatural. I swear the devil himself was her leader. She even claimed that she met with the devil often and that he gave her all of that power and strength. It all got to be a bit much for me, if you want to know the truth, sir!" The mayor felt like he was blubbering, as he wiped the sweat from his balding forehead.

"Oh, Mayor, did you ever see any symbol connected with the group?"

Mayor Casey remembered a ring that he had been given but had since disposed of. "Yes, sir, they do have a logo or something; it's a black eagle with a gold crown. I heard enough when I was around this bunch to know that they claim their organization is worldwide."

"Mayor, did you ever feel threatened by any members of the group?"

"Yes, I actually felt threatened all the time I was around any of them. I observed enough and had enough personal experience with them to know that you don't cross the people in this group. Well, wait a minute, I take that back. You'll be okay if you have *the light* shining in you. That's the light that the Murphys talked about."

President Roland made a mental note to ask about *the light* later, but he wanted a little more information first. "You said Lana gave you orders and I assume you obeyed them. What did you get in return?"

"The other guys and I were told that we would always have our jobs and never have any money problems if we cooperated with them. I was told I would receive extra money as long as I let them come here once a month to meet. The three of us would meet them with our limos and drive them to my house so they could use my big conference room for their meetings."

"Mayor, is Lana the only one of the group that you got to know?"

"Well, I couldn't say I even knew her, really, but I had very little to do with anyone else in the organization. I noticed that they talked only to Lana and I got my orders directly from Lana. The others never had a conversation with me and I stayed out of their way."

"Oh! I just remembered one more thing: these people never seemed to age! Isn't that odd? They never seemed to get a day older." The mayor's voice had taken on quite a casual, conversational tone, and when he noticed how comfortable he had become, he was a little taken aback. Better watch it, he thought.

"When you were driving them, did you ever hear them discuss any of their plans?"

51

"No, sir, never. I do know they have a lot of followers. And once I overheard them refer to someone as 'stupid humans'—as if to say *they* weren't."

The President was about to wrap up the conversation when he remembered the reference to light the mayor had made.

"By the way, Mayor, what shining light were you talking about?"

Mayor Casey had regained his confidence, so he sat up straight in his chair and boldly replied, "It's the beam of light that came into me when I received Jesus Christ as my personal savior. It is the Spirit of God that lives in me, Sir. JJ and Lynn told us all about it while they were here. Whenever that beam of light came into me, Lana and her whole group backed off and *were scared of me*. JJ and Lynn stayed over in Centerville long enough to teach us all about the light within us. I've started going to church regularly so I can understand it better."

DELAYED INVASION

7

The President thanked Mayor Casey, hung up the phone, and looked at Director Campbell.

"This confirms what you are telling me, Director. We are up against an organized group. I think I'll have the other men come in because we've got to get our heads together on this."

The President had Cindy usher in several of his top advisors who had been waiting in the reception area. He reiterated his conversation with Director Campbell and shared much of what he and Mayor Casey had discussed.

"These people comprise a religious cult who consider Satan their leader. They embrace some rather lofty ideals and their goal seems to be to rule the world and have us all worship the devil."

One of the advisors spoke up, "But what makes them different from dozens of other fanatical groups around the world?"

"Well," the President replied, "they have surreptitiously placed leaders in strategic locations worldwide and they also have infiltrated major corporations. Their leaders are extremely capable and while I had thought this was merely another run-of-the-mill group, we have to come to terms with the fact that this is a sinister, global operation. I don't think our agencies have ever been so duped before."

"I know Michael Adams' crew was killed. What do you know about that, Mr. President?"

"Sadly, I can confirm that. Michael's crew in Germany mysteriously tapped into a source of intelligence. Whether this was by chance or was skillful decoding, we don't know, although I knew they had an expert cryptographer on that crew. We do know, however, that whatever knowledge they uncovered led to their deaths."

"Director, can you shed any light on that?"

"Yes, we know that the five people who intercepted the plans for the worldwide catastrophe on the thirteenth knew they were in imminent danger. They fled the military base together to hide out, but they were all eliminated, shot to death."

The President continued, "I guess only Michael really knows what's going on. He was able to get a short message to me on my private line. His wife said that he was going to meet privately with someone of great importance and that he couldn't discuss it with her. She thought he might have set up a meeting with me. Come to think of it, that could have been the trick they used to get him to the place where he was abducted."

After several minutes of animated discussion, a military advisor spoke up, "We have been aware of these people and we located some of their members, but we never considered them a serious threat. And just to show you how good they are at covering their tracks, we had no idea they were operating all over the world. We must interrogate as many of them as we can immediately."

"Well, get to work! I know I don't have to impress on you that we have no time to waste. They have Michael and we have five dead members of the military, so if we didn't comprehend before how dangerous they are, WE DO NOW! This conspiracy clearly transcends party lines and political persuasions. Recruit anyone and everyone who can help!" The President then dismissed them.

As the men left the room, they noticed the President staring out the window, murmuring something under his breath, "This Satan-devil stuff is a total myth. How could intelligent world leaders fall for such ridiculous, illogical nonsense? It's absurd, absolutely absurd."

Claire Hollis, Ph.D.

DELAYED INVASION

8

L ana and her group were operating out of an old abandoned warehouse in what used to be a busy, profitable haven of heavy industry. Now an eerie stillness hung over the place. It was a maze of rusting railroad tracks, unoccupied foundries, machine shops, storage buildings, shipping and receiving ports with deteriorating hurricane fences, parking lots, and brooding structures that looked like bombed-out ruins in a war zone.

There was no hope here! In such an atmosphere, evil and gloom would feel right at home, camped out in the dark, deserted rooms and corridors of what was once a center of thriving business. All signs of prosperity were unwanted, forgotten, long dead.

But there was a party going on tonight! Lana and her evil counterparts were truly enjoying themselves as they celebrated their impending victory. Michael Adams could hear raucous laughter and obscene screams through the walls. Lana demanded silence, then loudly announced that she was leaving. As soon as she left, everyone went crazy! There was banging, laughing and singing, and occasionally Michael heard squeals that sounded like pigs.

Darkness was just setting in, and Michael had spent the day reading the Bible, squinting and straining to see by the meager light in his small prison area. It seemed like every page he read contained references to Satan and his kingdom of fallen angels. He did not know at that time that the Holy Spirit was directing his selection of scriptures. He could hardly believe what he was reading.

Even though Michael's father was a preacher, he had tuned out a lot of what he had heard as a child. Truthfully, the focal point of his father's messages had been the love of God and His grace and mercy toward the children He loved, but Satan got his share of "coverage" in the sermons.

Michael realized he had absorbed more than he thought, however, as he reflected on the story of Satan. Satan had been one of God's archangels, one of the most respected and trusted of all God's angels. But because of pride and lust for power, he turned his back on God, even trying to take God's place. He did a lot of talking, and through his deceptive persuasion, he convinced one-third of the angels in heaven to follow him. Because of this subversion, God kicked him out of heaven and he came to earth.

It was when God made the first man and woman and gave them dominion over the earth that Satan got mad and plotted to get revenge. He came to Adam and Eve in the Garden of Eden and deceived them, thus regaining authority and power. He is the prince of this world and ruler of the power of the air, and he has a countless number of helpers. Their only mandate is to kill, steal, and destroy. Since they don't die or sleep, they have twenty-four hours a day to deceive and wreak havoc on mankind.

When Jesus Christ, God's only Son, came down from His home in heaven and died for our sins, He went into hell and took the keys of death and hell away from Satan. Satan still had power, but he lost all his authority because of Jesus, Who died so that all mankind can know everlasting life in heaven.

Satan's plan is to become the leader of the world and have everyone worship *him*. He plans to bring peace to a world that is in chaos, establish a worldwide religion, and a worldwide money system. But it is a false peace, and God Almighty, Maker of heaven and earth and all that exists, will step in and foil the devil's evil plan. God and his chosen people will reign, and Satan will be thrown into a lake of fire.

Michael thought to himself, "Now I understand all the messages that were somehow intercepted. These demons plan to come to earth and pretend to be people from outer space. They plan to use their supernatural powers to take over the world."

Michael gazed at the Book in his hands. He had absorbed a lot of God's Word and he didn't know how long it would be before his captors checked on him. There was still just enough light for him to read, so he reached for the Bible again. To his astonishment, the Book seemed to fly open to a New Testament passage that almost jumped off the page at him. The verse was at the end of the book of Mark where Jesus was talking to His disciples. He was telling them that He was going away, but that He was leaving them, his disciples, ALL POWER OVER THE ENEMY. Michael knew that Jesus' words applied to him and all believers throughout the ages.

As Michael read these words, he remembered the beam of light that had disappeared into him and the peace that he knew had come from God. For some inexplicable reason, Michael Adams felt empowered, bold, and confident!

Michael had never heard the term "mental radiance" but he felt illumination hit his mind and he could almost visualize a radiant light inside his head. Even while trying to grasp all that was going on, he had instant understanding of the combat that he was engaged in.

"I'm a believer in Jesus Christ now," he thought. "Why should I take orders from Lana or any of her underlings? The God who just came into me was the same God who made those things out there in the other room. I should be giving *them* orders." Michael was truly walking in revelation and Holy Spirit power.

Michael could no longer read the Word because darkness had set in, but he could certainly think! And he could pray! "Oh, God, how could I have missed You? How could I have been so blind?"

Many of the stories Michael's father had told him returned as he sat in the darkness. He felt so foolish as what was once so complex and unbelievable became simple and plausible. Why now? Why had he waited this long to accept the truth? As if in answer to his question, his mind went back to what his father had always told him. He had insisted that there would come a time in Michael's life when he would *truly need God* and God would not forsake him. His father had promised that God would be there for him whenever Michael was ready to accept the truth. Ah, how wise his father had been.

Michael was in a reflective mood and he was able to block out the noise in the adjoining room enough to contemplate the significance of his decision to follow Christ. But as he pondered, he recognized that he was *feeling* emotions he had never felt before. He began to *feel* the light and love of God fill his spirit, his soul, the real Michael Adams! He didn't want these feelings washing over him to ever stop.

Again Michael was moved to cry out to God, "Oh, Father, how could I have forgotten You? In all the success I've had in my life, in the government position, in my marriage and children, in my finances, all of it, nothing is more exciting and satisfying than what I have experienced today." He smiled when he realized he hadn't even eaten and really hadn't thought about food. The people in the other room hadn't offered him anything, anyway.

"Lord, I don't feel alone anymore. How wonderful! I don't feel doomed to die here at the hands of these people or demons or whatever they are. I feel so blessed to finally *feel and know* what my father taught. I realize what love really is and what the light of God is all about. It's about the love of Jesus and the Holy Spirit that was sent to live inside of me. Thank you so much, Father."

Michael Adams was at peace! At peace with himself. At peace with the world. At peace with his Father.

The party in the next room was getting out of hand. The revelers were getting louder and he heard one of them yell, "Let's get the human out and have some fun with him!" When this "being" bolted through the door, anticipating some fun, what he saw stopped him in his tracks. He stared at Michael Adams, and screamed—a scream that could be heard all over the building! Immediately the rest of the bunch scurried to the door and peeked into the room. Even in the dim light, they could see what had startled their fellow demon. They screamed in unison at what they saw, shrank back, and grabbed their chests.

The first one to enter the room was now standing over Michael, yelling excitedly to the others, "He's got the light! I see it in him!" He took a few steps back, eyes bulging, as a hush came over the room. As one, they quickly retreated and closed the door. Michael could hear them talking just outside the room.

"Lana is going to be mad!"

"She's not just going to be mad—she's going to be *furious*!"

Their voices sounded anxious. "Lana is going to get us good because she'll think we didn't do our job. She'll accuse us of crossing her, and you know what happens when somebody crosses her! We're in big trouble!"

Another voice chimed in, "Personally, I think we should kill him and dispose of the body before Lana gets back. Why should we let her know what happened? It should be easy because there's no way that he can know about the power in him. He can't know he has power over us."

Michael picked up the Bible one last time and clutched it tightly near his heart. He remembered a phrase that he had read during the day about a believer being able to bind something on earth and it would be bound in heaven. He looked down at the Bible, concentrated, and tried to remember the phrase more precisely. "Help me, Lord," he breathed. He discerned that the verse meant that he had power over the demonic kingdom because of God's presence in him.

"They're going to kill me anyway, so what have I got to lose? Either this Book works or it doesn't!" He stood up, dusted himself off, and made a decision. "If Christ could walk into hell and ask Satan for his keys, then I should be able to walk through this group without fear. When Christ left the earth He said that we'll be able to do even greater things than He did!"

Armed with his newfound faith, Michael Adams felt a strength he had never felt before. He stood tall, squared his shoulders and put his hand on the doorknob. He then entered the room where evil reigned!

The party was over! The minute the revelers' eyes fell on him, their hearts turned to stone and their eyes mirrored sheer terror. Lifting both arms high above his head, Michael prominently displayed the treasured old Bible and bellowed, "I BIND YOU ALL IN THE NAME OF JESUS!"

What happened next defied all logic; he could hardly believe what was happening—and it was happening *through him!* Chains flew out of his fingertips and wrapped themselves around each demon, causing them to fall on the floor. They were bound from head to toe and Michael watched as they squirmed and jerked, trying to escape their shackles. Realizing the futility of their efforts, they snarled, cursed, slobbered, and made very strange sounds. Many of them were thrashing about the floor, exposing their teeth like mad dogs.

Michael made his way carefully through the writhing bodies on the floor, carefully dropped the Bible just inside the room, opened the door, and walked out into the night. Gulping deep breaths of the cool, fresh air, he raced through the gloom of the deserted area, looking for help. He had to contact the President and let him know what was going on.

Thank God! A pay phone! Reaching into his pocket for change, to his chagrin, Michael found that he had no coins. What now? "God, help me!"

Glancing down at the trash-strewn pavement, Michael saw something glistening—coins! Miraculously, it seemed, enough change to make his call was there for him. He had tried to comprehend all that was happening, but it was so mind-boggling that he gave up. "Just accept it, Michael. This whole thing is bigger than you. Someone else is in charge."

Michael quickly dialed a private number, the direct line into the President's office. A very nervous and worried President grabbed the phone and went limp with relief when he heard Michael's voice.

"Michael! Thank God! Where are you?"

The President listened for a few moments, then interrupted, "OK, someone will be there within minutes. They're tracing the call right now and it won't be difficult to locate you."

Michael fidgeted as he waited. Although it was only about ten minutes, it seemed like a lifetime before the federal agents arrived to pick him up. He was surprised to find that he had not been taken outside the city limits.

Within the hour Michael was escorted into the President's office. The President stood up, whirled around, and ran over to Michael.

The men embraced like close friends who had not seen each other in years instead of hours. The personnel in the room turned away to afford them privacy.

"Man, am I ever glad to see you! How on earth did you escape?"

Michael looked at his friend and was horrified to see how haggard he looked. President Roland looked like he had aged ten years and his eyes were red from lack of sleep. It was obvious he hadn't shaved, and his brown, wavy hair was a mess.

Strangely, the Secretary of Defense seemed calm and very much at peace, *now that he had escaped!* Could this be the peace that the Bible described as "peace that surpasses understanding?"

"Mr. President, it's a story you'll never believe!"

"Try me, Michael!" said the President. "I've heard things today so unbelievable that I don't think I can be shocked anymore."

Michael began his story with facts the President already knew, but was able to add new details.

The crew in Germany somehow unknowingly tapped into an unknown frequency, later proven to be the supernatural realm. Demon spirits were discussing how they would invade the earth disguised as people from outer space. The target date for the invasion was the thirteenth and the target location was the entire world. They would land in space ships and although people would be curious and interested, they would not realize the danger the beings posed.

"The crew was able to determine that the report was not a hoax, and that's when they reported to me directly."

"Did you tell them to get out of there?" the President asked.

"Oh, yes! I instructed them to leave as quickly as possible and get to someplace safe. Their safety was of utmost importance—a priority! They were to get back to me only after they had achieved safe passage."

Michael further explained to the President that before the crew shut down all the equipment, they intercepted one last message that let them know the demons were aware of their identities and their whereabouts. An alert went out that these men were to be eliminated at all costs.

White House staff brought in food at the President's directive, and as he watched the half-starved Secretary of Defense eat, he couldn't refrain from asking more questions.

"What about the woman? Where does she fit into all this? I called some people and they told some pretty wild stories about her."

Between bites, Michael continued. "The woman named Lana got my private home number and called me quite early in the morning. She told me to meet her at a used car lot near 14th and Eisenhower because she had a message for me from the crew. She emphasized that it was top-secret information that could help save the world."

The President's attention was riveted on Michael's every word and he tried to hide his alarm as Michael continued.

"Lana told me that she knew all about the plot to take over the world and to kill my men, and she could help, but she had to meet with me. She insisted that I come alone. Then she told me, 'Mr. Adams, you absolutely must tell no one where you are going. And do not even speak of this phone call.' She made it all sound very mysterious."

"Was Carol at home when you got the call?"

"Yes, she was in the room, now that I think of it. She had a questioning look on her face as I was talking, but she's accustomed to the calls at home. She did ask me what it was about, but I tried to appear casual about it. I really need to call her right away!"

"Absolutely, Michael. In fact, I'll have Cindy call Carol and tell her you're safe and will call her just as soon as this debriefing is over." Michael nodded his gratitude. The President asked Cindy to join them in the Oval Office after she made the call.

"Well, let's see, where were we? The woman said that if I didn't come alone, I would never see her or hear from her again. And here's the strange part. That phone call could not be traced and there was no record of it having been made. It's as if it never came through the wire."

Michael paused, seemingly collecting his thoughts. "When I got there. something inside warned me that this was a set-up. I tried to appear nonchalant and walk quickly away, but two men came out of nowhere. As soon as I saw them, I started to run but, hey, their guns spoke loud and clear! I'll admit I was terrified! Before I could even think, a limousine drove up, pulled to the curb, and I was cornered."

Michael was animated as he continued, "This helpless-looking, tiny woman picked me up like I was a pretzel and tossed me into the limo. It was the wildest thing I've ever experienced. The guys with the guns were getting in the limo and this little woman with superhuman strength was taking charge of everything. She blindfolded me and they drove off. We ended up somewhere on the west side of town in an old, abandoned building. It was pretty awful in there, but I managed to escape and call you from the phone booth."

The President sat spellbound, and asked, "How did you escape?"

Michael took another bite of food and a sip of coffee. "Well, sir, I guarantee you one thing ... you're not going to believe the rest of this story."

A look of concern crossed Michael's face as he said, "Excuse me, Mr. President, but it is true that my crew is dead?".

The President hung his head, "Yes, Michael, I'm so sorry. They were all found dead." The President hesitated a moment as he heard Michael gasp. "Please finish telling me how you got away," he said softly.

Michael bowed his head and was visibly upset over the group killing. However, he had to continue, so he breathed a prayer and regained his composure.

"Mr. President, this is so hard to explain. I saw and heard things that are totally unbelievable. They defy explanation and human logic. I saw men who were stuck up on a wall just by a look from this Lana woman; then they disappeared through the wall! I couldn't believe my eyes!"

Michael had regained his energy and was in his famous (or infamous, according to his friends) storytelling mode.

"They stuck me in a dark room by myself and told me I would never see Carol or the kids again. They threatened to kill me, as well, and believe me, I was scared. They were very convincing. I don't know if I ever told you, but my dad was a preacher, although I know I've never acted like I had any religious training. But death threats have a way of making you think! So I prayed in that room. I fell on my knees and I cried out to God, 'If you're real, God, then show yourself to me.' I think I've always known He was real, but I was in rebellion and running from Him."

The President sat straighter in his chair, rapt with attention. Was this really his friend talking?

"Through the years I've joked about having an epiphany now and then when I got a bright idea. But the only way I can explain what happened next is that it was *truly* an epiphany. I told the Lord that I believe He is real and that I believe that He sent His only Son Jesus Christ to die for my sins. I told Him that if He would forgive my sins, I would serve Him forever. And I know He heard me! We sealed the bargain! That's when the beam of light, so bright that I could see it through my closed eyes, came into the room where I was."

Michael could see that his story was having a strange effect on the President. "Wait! That's not all! The beam of light entered my chest and a man appeared in the room, a man about ten feel tall, with a sword in his hand. I know, I know, it sounds weird. But it happened! The man showed me where there was a Bible hidden in the wall and I took it out and read it all day. I seemed to find a lot of scriptures about Satan and his kingdom, but I also read that a person who has accepted Christ as Savior has authority over Satan and his demons. I felt really bold and confident, so I walked into the room where all the demons were and yelled as loudly as I could, 'I bind you all in Jesus' Name.' To my surprise, the strangest thing happened. (The President was thinking, how could things get any stranger?) The demons suddenly had chains around them, and they all fell to the floor, trying to get loose. Lana wasn't there, so I ran out and didn't stop until I found a pay phone and called you."

The President shook his head in disbelief. By now the story had become so preposterous that it was becoming rather ridiculous and he had to suppress a smile. He could accept the story about God, but the demon stuff was a little more than he could handle. Cindy was a strong Christian, however, and she knew exactly what Michael was talking about. Michael took comfort in the fact that he knew she was silently praying for him.

The four men left the room because they could not hold back their chuckles. They gathered in the hallway and broke out in laughter. "Michael Adams has definitely lost it! I wonder who will take his place. He'll be locked up in a psychiatric ward by morning," one of them said.

Another chimed in, "And to think we got called in for something like this! It's absolutely nuts! Some national emergency! A bunch of religious kooks! I'm going to see if I can go home! What about you guys?"

They continued to make fun of the situation as they left the White House and went to a favorite hangout.

The President walked over to the window and stared out, absorbed in thought. He had an awful lot of information to digest. Cindy and Michael sat on the long couch and talked in low voices. Silently they prayed for their friend and President.

"Michael seems so sincere about all this demon and beam of light and Bible stuff," the President thought. "Is there really anything to this? Have my political ambitions buried my spiritual inclinations? God, have I completely ignored You?" He quickly dismissed these musings with a shake of his head and resolved to keep his mind on the matters at hand: the threat that this woman Lana and her group posed.

DELAYED INVASION

9

Lana's driver let her out in front of the abandoned warehouse and parked the limousine. Throwing open the door and striding in with her customary self-assurance, she was immobilized with outrage as she saw the demons on the floor, squirming and thrashing about, unable to get up. They were desperately crying out in pain and fear.

"What's going on here?" she screeched. Her driver could hear her screaming all the way outside. She ran into the room where Michael Adams had been and found it empty. Frantically retracing her steps, she started to leave the building when she spotted the Bible on the floor where Michael had dropped it. Realizing immediately what had happened, she glanced down at the Book. The front cover flew open and she saw some words written in large letters that read, "YOU HAVE ALL POWER OVER THE ENEMY."

Enraged, Lana stormed around the room, snatching up her underlings as easily as she would pluck flowers off a bush. They were crying and trembling so hard that their teeth chattered. Infuriated by their failure to hold Michael Adams prisoner, Lana hurled each one straight through the ceiling, through the roof, and out of this world into the void. Who knows where they landed? It was surely a place humans knew nothing about.

She slammed the door and bolted out to the waiting car. The driver was shaking, fearful for his own safety after what he had just witnessed.

Picking up the car phone, Lana launched into an animated conversation and the driver could easily hear what she was saying.

"It's Lana. I'm checking in as you asked, my lord. We're on schedule. The space ships are all in place. Everyone will transform themselves into outer space beings at midnight tonight. The invasion is planned for tomorrow, Wednesday, the thirteenth, when the sun is at midday over the United States. You'll be sitting on your throne within the week. My lord, with your permission, I want to erect a statue of you in the place that God calls the Holy City."

Lana listened intently to the words of her master before replying, "I'm glad you're pleased with my idea. I thought you'd like it. In just days everybody on earth will be eating out of your hand. My lord, when you called me here to Washington I thought my job would only be to get rid of all the Christians. I am truly honored that you chose me and trusted in me to fulfill this mission. Your plan is brilliant, but there is just one thing I don't understand. We will be able to control the entire world except for the Christians. What do you want us to do about them? Even though they are only a small percentage of the earth's population, I need to know how to handle them."

Lana was quiet for a few minutes then broke into peals of evil, hideous laughter that pierced the ears of the limo driver. He was one of her own but beads of sweat were breaking out on his forehead, because he didn't know his fate. He remembered how easily Lana had dealt with his companions and it struck fear in his heart.

"You're so right, my master! Only a few of those Christians even know about or realize the authority that God has given to them. You're right, of course. We don't have a problem. As long as they don't realize the power they have over us, then we can totally control them. This is great!" Lana sounded gleeful as she talked.

Lana continued to praise her leader. "You've done all the groundwork and you've done it like a true master. You have made the subject of deliverance look so foolish and fearsome that pastors, evangelists, and priests have been afraid to teach their people about it. You've been able to get Christians to rise up against anyone who tries to teach on the subject. I love the phrase you designed and embedded in Christian leaders all over the world: 'Don't say anything about the devil, don't give him any glory!' What a plan! Master, you are a genius!" Again Lana fairly exploded into giddy, evil laughter.

"My lord, one other minor detail. We could have a potential problem. Remember Reverend JJ and Lynn Murphy from Centerville? I didn't mention this to you before because I didn't know if it was significant, but they have written a book entitled *This Means War!* That book exposes our kingdom and teaches Christians how to expel us out of their lives. It also teaches them how to bind up our powers and render us inactive. My lord, that one book could put us out of business if it ever gets published. These two seem to have more influence than we realized and I think they have the potential of influencing millions. They caused us so much grief in Centerville that we had to quit meeting there."

The voice at the other end of the line seemed to explode and the driver was shocked that he could hear every word. He imagined he felt the car shake. "FIND THEM! FIND THE BOOK! AND DESTROY THEM BOTH! AND I MEAN NOW!"

Lana was instructed to postpone the invasion until she had completed this assignment. "Yes, my lord. Yes, we will make sure that Michael Adams dies first. You can count on it!"

Lana shuddered as she hung up the phone. With trembling hands she pushed a button that connected her to other leaders in her classified group, which was headquartered right in Washington, D.C. All told, thirteen stronghold forces were in charge of many other demon forces and agents around the world.

Lana shouted into the phone, "Send out all our forces and find the manuscript that JJ and Lynn Murphy wrote while they were in Centerville. I want immediate action! The whole invasion of earth is on hold until we destroy that manuscript. Use everything and every method at your disposal to destroy them. I HATE THEM AND OUR LEADER HATES THEM, TOO. Get rid of them at any cost, and I mean NOW! I also want you to find Michael Adams and bring him to me alive!"

Lana shouted one more command, "Meet me at our new location at seven o'clock in the morning and you'd better have some good reports by then!" She slammed down the phone, and slumped into the seat, totally spent.

Claire Hollis, Ph.D.

DELAYED INVASION

10

C indy left the room and the President and Michael Adams continued to talk.

"Michael, we've known each other a long time and I really want to believe you, but this story you're telling is really farfetched. It's so implausible that I don't know how to digest it or what to do with it. I can't very well get on national TV and say that demons are going to invade our planet disguised as beings from outer space. I can't do that! The media would crucify me!" Michael realized that the idea of crucifixion held a new, deeper meaning for him.

The President went on, "We *must* warn the nation, however. I've had your family under surveillance and

I'm sending you all to a safe house that even you don't know about—we call it the compound. There is a couple there already, Reverend and Mrs. JJ Murphy, and they have had their own personal encounters with the woman named Lana. You should all have a good time comparing notes."

Michael lifted his hand as though to protest, but the President was insistent. "Don't argue, Michael. Carol and the children are ready and a helicopter is waiting for you on the lawn right now." Michael's spirits lifted at the thought of seeing his family.

"I'll talk to you tomorrow, Michael. I'm so incredibly glad that you're alive. I must admit I'm a little concerned about the effects the kidnapping has had on you, but I think you'll soon come to your senses. I need you back at work! Go now! You need rest and now maybe I can get a little rest myself," the beleaguered leader of the free world told his Secretary of Defense.

Just before he left the Oval Office, Michael turned to look his friend directly in the eyes, "Mr. President, you and I have been with each other in this political game for a long time. We've won some and we've lost some, but in the last few hours, I've won the most vital battle of my life. I'll be praying tonight that you win yours."

Michael continued, "And I'm not talking about the invasion conspiracy, either, Mr. President. You know what I'm talking about. I love you, my friend, and God loves you."

Michael turned, exited, and joined the military escort awaiting him in the reception area. Cindy looked at him as he made his way out and gave him a very subtle "thumbs up." He smiled and returned the gesture.

The President was so exhausted he could barely think but he went to his favorite window and watched Michael board the helicopter waiting on the White House lawn.

On his way to his private living quarters, he allowed his thoughts to wander back over some of the revelations Michael had shared. Angels? Demons? A beam of light from God? A man ten feet tall? Fascinating, spellbinding stuff, he thought. But what was he to think of Michael's newfound faith? That surprised and intrigued him more than anything else.

"Well, I'll get some rest. Then things will look clearer, I'm sure." The President was talking to himself as he made his way to the bedroom. He lay down without getting under the covers and was fast asleep as soon as his head hit the pillow. The First Lady, only napping, was relieved to see her spouse finally take a break from all the stress. She worried about him so much and wished she could help in some way, but she knew very little about this latest crisis.

Claire Hollis, Ph.D.

DELAYED INVASION

11

B ack in his office, President Peter Roland felt completely refreshed after a two-hour rest, a quick shower, and a change of clothes. He didn't realize that he had had dreams about angels and a beautiful place filled with love and peace. A place where God's love ruled.

Reaching for JJ's manuscript, he read the title: *This Means War!* Interesting title, he thought. He began to read and before he knew it, he was totally engrossed in the work. It took a couple of hours, but he had his staff hold all calls and he read the entire manuscript from beginning to end. Reading the book opened up a lot of his understanding, and he wondered if he might have been too harsh on Michael when he questioned his mental state after the kidnapping.

The President slightly shook his head, as if to clear his mind, and thought for several minutes. Then he did something he hadn't done since election night (when he desperately wanted to win!). He prayed! And this time his prayer was sincere.

"God, I've heard a lot about you in the last couple of days," President Roland prayed to a Father Who had *always* been there. "I'm not real sure what to make of all this. Reverend Murphy, Lana, Mayor Casey at Centerville...Michael, the military crew...and now this book. God, if You are real, I want you in my life. Please give me what Michael talked about. I really do want to believe. I know I've always secretly laughed at believers and ridiculed the Bible, but now, God, I think I understand it. I don't know why, but it's beginning to make sense to me."

Something was stirring in the President's heart and he thought of Reverend Murphy and his wife. How could such peaceful people know so much about warfare? They seemed compassionate and concerned about people and they obviously were unusual. Love radiated from them, yet they were strong and stable. Why did people have the notion that Christians were cowardly or powerless, needing a crutch?

The President then thought of Michael, his dear and trusted friend. There was certainly nothing weak or flaky about Michael but he had wholly embraced the message of Jesus Christ. And he seemed like a different person.

"Father, I believe! I *choose* to believe that You sent Jesus to die for the sins I've committed. I understand that that was the only option You had for saving humanity from Satan's hold over us. Michael seemed so changed, God, and I want that change in my life. I like what I saw in Michael, Lord. I thank You right now, Jesus, for forgiving everything I have ever done to displease You. Wash me clean with the blood that Jesus shed on the cross at Calvary, and fill me with the power of your Holy Spirit."

President Roland leaned forward and rested his head on his desk. "Help me, God! I need Your help in order to properly lead this country. I need Your help and guidance during this crisis. Give me wisdom, Lord."

He didn't realize his head was resting on JJ Murphy's manuscript. And with his eyes closed, he didn't see the beam of light that came through the ceiling and disappeared inside him. He didn't see it, but he felt it! Something dramatic had happened to him! He jumped up from his desk and called to Cindy, who was sound asleep sitting in the chair at her desk in the next room. Sometimes she was at the office twenty-four hours a day, especially in times of crisis.

"Cindy! Cindy, come in here! I've got some good news!"

Cindy grabbed her laptop computer and ran to see what the President wanted.

"Cindy, I think I have just been born again!" He could hardly believe what he was saying. The term "born again" had become so closely associated with fanatical "religious right" groups that it was going to require a mental adjustment for him to think of it in spiritual terms. But it was biblical! Jesus had told the "rich young ruler" in the Book of John that he must be *born again* in order to enter heaven.

Cindy burst out, "Hallelujah! That's wonderful news, Mr. President. Praise the Lord!" She could not contain her joy, and her exuberance almost embarrassed the President. Some of the other staff heard the commotion and looked through the door at the two of them

"I think I see and understand the plot of the enemy now. This manuscript really put things in perspective and helped me get a picture of the plans Satan has for this world. This book must get into the hands of the people. I want you to get Matthew Monroe on the phone. He owns Nationwide Publishing, the biggest publishing house in the country, but before you call him, have several copies of this disk made. We must hide them just as a precaution, because I don't want anything to happen to them. I'm going to have Monroe immediately publish Reverend Murphy's book and get it shipped all over the country. *This Means War!* is going to be an instant bestseller! Oh, by the way, get extra security agents in here immediately and arrange to have at least fifty helicopters lined up."

A beaming Cindy set out to do the bidding of her President, who was now a *man of God!* She got Mr. Monroe on the phone and put him through to the President.

"Mr. Monroe, sorry to wake you up in the middle of the night, but I have an urgent request. Oh, by the way, this is President Roland. Yes, it really is. Listen, we have an urgent matter that I need to discuss with you."

A drowsy Matthew Monroe quickly became alert and responded to President Roland. "Yes, sir! Now I recognize your voice. I would be happy to assist you in any way possible."

"I have a manuscript in my hands that must be published right away and distributed to every book-store in the country immediately. I know you are a man of influence and I authorize you to use any resources you see fit. You will have access to any and every printing press in this country. We are going to have it translated in every known language and dialect, then distributed in foreign lands, as well."

Matthew Monroe was furiously taking notes, trying to comprehend the enormity of the request (command?) the President was presenting.

"This is top priority, Mr. Monroe. You will have the military at your command. We already have people on this project—the translators are at work, paper companies, adjunct printers, charter planes and other services have been notified. A lot of people are being hauled out of bed even as we speak. But this is a matter of national security, and it also is top priority. The manuscript is entitled *This Means War!* and will be at your door within the hour. I already have authorized one hundred skilled men and women to be at your office when you get there, so don't be shocked. General Joshua Rushing is in command and will be in charge of the personnel. They will make phone calls, transport materials or whatever you need."

A rather startled Matthew Monroe replied, "Yes, sir, Mr. President. I appreciate your confidence. I am honored. We will put forth every effort to have this manuscript out to the public tomorrow, if that's what you need."

President Roland finished talking to this surprised, motivated and capable publisher, and immediately turned his attention to other matters. One of the attributes that made him such an effective leader was his ability to detach and disengage from one situation and totally concentrate on another. He buzzed Cindy, who was at her desk putting presidential requests into action.

"Cindy, call the media department and have them notify all national and international outlets that a press conference is scheduled for seven o'clock. Preempt all, and I mean *all*, regular radio and television programming in the morning, then call the compound and get the Murphys and Michael Adams on the phone for me."

Cindy had never known the President to act so swifty, so decisively, even in times of crisis, but she was observing a new, more courageous and confident President. And she knew exactly why it was happening now!

DELAYED INVASION

12

JJ and Lynn had spent the day in prayer and were excited when they heard that Michael Adams and his family were being brought to the compound.

"It sure will be nice to get Michael Adams' perspective on things, won't it?"

JJ and Lynn met Michael, Carol, and their children in a large, luxurious room filled with deep, leather couches, two fireplaces, a billiards table, a conference table, a bank of arcades for the children and every imaginable amusement and comfort. JJ and Lynn were struck by the dignity and charm of the entire family. Although the children were spoiled, they had good social graces.

JJ and Lynn engaged in animated conversation with Michael, comparing notes about Lana. And Michael shared that Carol and the children were fascinated with spiritual things. They saw such a remarkable difference in Michael that they were eager to hear everything he said. Even though some of the things he told them seemed like fiction, they trusted him. Michael told JJ and Lynn that he felt Carol and the children were open to the message of salvation.

Lynn asked Carol and the children to join her around a small table where they talked about Jesus and the plan of salvation. They all had a basic knowledge of Christ, the crucifixion and resurrection, but they had many questions. Lynn asked JJ and Michael to join them in prayer as Carol and the two children confessed their sins and asked Jesus to become the lord of their lives.

When they finished praying, three beams of light entered the room and disappeared into them.

During the day, the four ever-present security officers had spoken with JJ and Lynn several times and asked very astute questions. A couple of them seemed deeply interested in spiritual things and all four of them were watching and listening to the conversation that was taking place right now. When they saw the beams of light enter Carol and the children, they fell on their knees and begged JJ to pray for them to receive Christ. What a day of rejoicing! The compound had become like a cathedral of praise, totally obliterating any thought of the chaos and impending disaster outside.

Just as JJ finished praying, the red phone rang! Before he said anything to JJ, The President requested that he be put on the speakerphone that rang throughout the compound.

"Reverend Murphy, I read your manuscript and was *born again* as a result. I believe all the things you said about demons and their power and how we can overcome them. Do you recall my telling you when you missed your appointment with your publisher friend that I would see to it that your manuscript was published? Well, I have great news for you! The book is being printed as we speak, and by tomorrow it will be available to everyone in the United States. It is also being translated and will be distributed worldwide within days."

JJ's mouth almost fell open! "Oh, Reverend Murphy, is Michael there with you?"

"Yes, Mr. President, he's right here."

"Good, good. I'm going to call a press conference at seven o'clock in the morning and I want you and Michael to be here. Plans are already in place to get you here on time. I am going to promote this book and recommend that every citizen in the nation read it. Michael, I will want you to release to the media every bit of data that your crew intercepted. I realize now that you don't need to be in hiding from Lana. You have authority over her—she retreats every time you come around. It was my mistake for sending you away, but I just didn't know enough at the time to make a sound judgment. Sorry!" The President paused.

"Reverend Murphy, thank you for giving me your manuscript. I can't possibly put into words what reading it has…"

"Mr. President," JJ interrupted, "please. I can't accept your thanks. All praise goes to our heavenly Father, not to the man who wrote the book. Without the wisdom of the Lord and His inspiration and guidance, the book never would have been written. It is I who must thank you for accepting what you read. And I am so thankful that you have arranged to get His words out to the public."

Michael broke in, "I think you might be interested to know that everyone in this room has been born again—my family and all your personnel."

"My God," exclaimed President Roland. "This thing is big! Bigger than all of us! Let's all go to work. This time we're going to be working for God's kingdom. Let's see if we can mess up the devil's kingdom! We're in a battle, that's for certain. It may be an unseen battle, but we are on the side that wins. These unseen forces aren't going to win this war! Reverend, Michael, everyone there who believes in Jesus, we have the power! Now let's use it!" The staff in the compound could hardly believe what they were hearing, but their spirits were lifted. They could hardly wait to obtain their personal copy of *This Means War!*

DELAYED INVASION

13

Riding along in the limo, Lana meditated on the words of Satan, her master. She was terrified at how he would punish her once he found out that Michael Adams had escaped. What terrified her further was the fact that Adams had *the light* in him. Her concentration was broken when her periphery vision caught the sight of flashing red lights. She jerked her head up and saw at once that her car was surrounded. She was almost knocked to the floor as her driver slammed on the brakes!

"Come on! Let's get out of here!" she shouted to the driver. The sound of Lana's voice still echoed in the car as a powerful gust of wind blew through the limousine. Quicker than the eye could comprehend, Lana and the driver were gone. *Vanished!*

Local police, the FBI, the National Guard and private security agents had been planning this apprehension meticulously for days. They had been following Lana's car for several miles and had everyone in place for the actual capture.

Slowly inching their way toward the limo, they fingered their guns. When they got to the car, however, they couldn't spot the driver or Lana and one of the agents warned, "Careful! They must be on the floor."

Cautiously, several men and a couple of women drew closer to the limousine, glancing in the windows. The windows were tinted, so someone carefully tried one of the doors. To their surprise, the door opened! They scrambled around looking for Lana and the driver, but couldn't believe what they were *not* seeing. There was no Lana and there was no driver in that car!

Standing outside the car scratching their heads, the officers looked befuddled. They definitely had seen the driver in that limo—there was no mistake about that. But there also was no mistake that two people had vanished right before their eye.

"Let's take another look! Maybe we missed something." They returned to the car and to their complete amazement, they realized they *had* missed something. On the driver's seat lay a pile of clothes and a chauffeur's cap. On the back seat lay a bright red dress and a long, black coat with fur on the collar and cuffs.

Acting on information obtained from Michael Adams and other sources, a special task force had taken on the difficult assignment of locating Lana. They had traced her to the hideout in the deserted industrial complex and concluded that she had fled in the same black limo that had been used in Michael's abduction. Through careful coordination of the various federal agencies, they had ID'd the car, set up a roadblock, and felt very confident of success. Now this! How can you explain a disappearance that happens right in front of your eyes? There had been somebody in that car—cars don't just drive themselves, for heaven's sake!

The officer in charge dreaded what he had to do. "If this situation weren't so serious, it would be comical," he thought. But it was serious and he *had to make this call.*

"Mr. President, we had them, but somehow…well, you won't believe this, sir, but *somehow* they disappeared into thin air. There was a driver in the front and a woman in the back. We could see the driver when the car stopped. We can't be certain the woman was in the car because of the tinted windows, but we smelled her perfume and found a pile of clothes like she wore." The officer was embarrassed.

"Yes, sir, it's the same vehicle. Dent in the left rear fender and a bumper sticker with a black eagle wearing a gold crown. Forensics is going over the limo right now. Where do we go from here?"

The President spoke, and the officer answered, "I assure you, sir, they are not around here anyplace. Our spotlights were on them and we could see into the front of the car. I'm telling you, sir, the driver just disappeared right in front of our eyes. We all saw it! It was weird, right out of a horror movie—real-life special effects." The officer sounded bewildered.

"Excuse me, Mr. President. The preliminary forensics report is here. The only fingerprints on the car anywhere, inside or out, belong to Michael Adams. There aren't even any prints on the steering wheel. No, sir! The driver was not wearing gloves. Beats me, sir. We'll wait to hear further from you."

The officer turned and joined the other befuddled agents.

DELAYED INVASION

14

The atmosphere of the compound was charged with excitement and anticipation. JJ and Lynn hummed as they felt the joy of the events with Michaels' family. They were also a little apprehensive about having to appear on national television with the President.

"What am I going to wear? I didn't bring any decent clothes with me. I thought we were just going to meet with your buddy about the book."

Lynn saw a knowing expression cross JJ's face. Picking up the telephone, he said, "I imagine they have it all covered, Honey. Let's try to guess what your outfit is going to look like."

"Would you be able to get some clothes for my wife to wear to the press conference this morning? She didn't come prepared to appear in public."

"No problem at all sir, we have a section of the house set aside for this. It is like a fine department store. Give us her sizes and color preferences and we'll take care of her."

About twenty minutes later there was a knock on the door and the man brought in five complete outfits on a rack, smiled, and left. There were undergarments, handbags, shoes and assorted accessories.

The Murphys looked at the designer clothes, looked at one another, then laughed. As she fingered the assortment of Armani, Dana Buchman, Ralph Lauren and Donna Karan suits, Lynn jokingly told her husband, "I'm going to really miss this place!" JJ cast a wistful look at the closet where his simple suit hung.

After choosing an outfit and wishing she could dress like that all the time, Lynn quietly looked at JJ. Even though she said nothing, JJ knew exactly what his wife was thinking. They reached out to each other, then knelt beside the bed.

JJ began, "Thank You! Thank You! What a wonderful, loving Father You are, God. You are so good to all of us and we thank You for the opportunity to serve You. The book truly is Yours, not ours! We're thankful that You chose us to write it. Thank You so much for the President's salvation. Thank You for the power You grant us over the enemy. Thank You for life itself, and let us be worthy so that one day

You will say, 'Well done, good and faithful servant. Come on in!'"

It was Lynn's turn to pray. "We bind you, Satan, your power, your authority, and your kingdom. In the Name of Jesus, we command that you cannot and will not influence or hinder this press conference or the publishing of *This Means War!* Heavenly Father, please station mighty warring angels around us and the President, and Michael Adams and his family. Keep us from all harm from the demonic kingdom. God, have your angels encamp around these books and hold back the forces of Satan and his kingdom from hindering the publishing and the distribution. We ask you, heavenly Father, that those who read the book will be set free of any evil influence in their lives, and that they will understand the demonic kingdom and begin to take authority over it."

Lynn finished praying and with one voice, the Murphys said, "In Jesus' Name we pray. Amen!" They knelt for a moment more, never seeing the beam of light that shone around them. They just knew for sure that God's love and grace surrounded them.

Claire Hollis, Ph.D.

DELAYED INVASION

15

President Roland entered the room smiling, appearing at least ten years younger than he had yesterday. Everyone rose as he came into the room. The media had come out in force to see what had precipitated this impromptu press conference. They were buoyed to observe the President's seemingly calm demeanor. This was not his style, some of them thought, as they prepared to take notes.

The President told JJ, Lynn, and Michael to stay backstage until he called for them.

"Let me preface this press conference by saying that I know I may become the laughingstock of the nation when we're done here, but just wait until everyone gets a copy of the new book entitled *This Means War!* We'll try to prepare you for what's coming and answer some of the inevitable questions. I'll be introducing some unannounced panelists to you, because they may be able to shed light on subjects I know little or nothing about."

The President had told Michael and the Murphys earlier that they may be ridiculed and mocked by the media, but they were prepared. However, they didn't want to go onstage any earlier than was necessary.

The President continued, "I request that you show respect for those whom I will call upon to appear before you people assembled here in this room and you citizens watching by television. I am aware that this morning's press conference will strike many of you as unusual, and I am also aware that some will even accuse me of breaking the law. On that note, I am asking Reverend JJ Murphy to lead us in prayer."

Looking out over the audience, the President could see that members of the press were obviously mystified and disturbed. Their faces mirrored anxiety and fear, and their eyes were cold. Mouths fell open when he mentioned prayer, because that seemed to blur the lines in the "church/state" division issue. "What could the President possibly be talking about? And what's this business about prayer?" President Roland could be crossing the line here. The media was poised to strike; the room was abuzz.

The members of the media were too stunned to offer much resistance, so when JJ stepped forward, they respectfully bowed their heads while he prayed a short prayer.

They had heard faint rumors of an impending disaster, so they hoped they would get some of this cleared up.

"Thank you, Reverend Murphy," the President murmured. "Ladies and gentlemen, you all know our esteemed Secretary of Defense and you heard about his kidnapping. Well, I am happy to report that he is safe—and, in fact, he is here with us today."

A loud gasp filled the room and surprise and shock registered on the faces of everyone as Michael Adams walked through the door. Spontaneous applause exploded and the grim expressions turned to wide smiles. They had no idea that he had escaped, and they began shouting questions at him. He responded calmly, and a glow seemed to emanate from his smile.

DELAYED INVASION

16

L ana's lieutenants were in their seats waiting as she entered the room. They had been watching television when a "special bulletin" notice filled the screen. Someone pressed the "mute" button so they could give their full attention to their leader.

Lana's petite frame whipped to the the head table and she stood and faced her captive audience. She was making a hissing sound, which gave way to growling. When she opened her mouth, fangs appeared, and she momentarily looked like a mad dog. Not a pretty sight! She pounded her fist on the table, splitting it down the center with a resounding crash, and her underlings scattered in terror. Some of them knocked over chairs in their mad dash to avoid her wrath.

"Get your reports out immediately! They had better be good!" she barked loudly. Hissing, growling, barking. This evil woman had a whole arsenal of noises and expressions with which to intimidate and control. She had two dresses that she alternated, one red and one black. Today she was wearing the black one, and her hair was styled in her usual chignon. She was a stylish woman who was quite attractive when she wasn't angry.

Lana's wretched cohorts put their chairs back into a semblance of order, because the table was now useless, and sat down. Their faces were drawn and haggard, and they knew that they had only seen the first of several outbursts that day. Dread!

One of Lana's operatives spoke up, "I've tried to find Michael Adams, but he and his family disappeared without a trace. There is absolutely no trail to follow." He quickly sat down.

A second one stood. "The same can be said of the Murphys. They are nowhere to be found"

Yet another rose. "About the manuscript of *This Means War!* it seems like..." he started, but something on the television captured their attention.

The room grew completely silent and they all turned toward Lana to see her reaction. She started to splutter, her face turned bright red, and she looked apoplectic.

"Turn on the sound!" she screamed as she saw the face of her enemy fill the screen.

DELAYED INVASION

17

A ll eyes were on Michael Adams as he raised his hands and asked for quiet in the room. "Ladies and gentlemen of the press and citizens of the United States and the world, I thank you for giving us your attention this morning."

The press sat in rapt attention as the Secretary of Defense continued, "Before President Roland returns, I want to thank the Lord for my safe return from a perilous situation. No one was hurt in my escape and I feel truly blessed. I thank God for saving my life. I must ask you, however, to forego any questions directly relating to my escape, because much more pressing matters are before us."

After fielding several general questions, Michael felt he had said enough.

Turning toward President Roland, Michael introduced his Commander-in-Chief loudly, "Ladies and gentlemen, the President of the United States."

The President quickly stepped forward again and began, "Ladies and gentlemen of the press and citizens everywhere, recently our defense department intercepted information from a source not known to this planet."

The sound of whispering filled the room. The President continued, "The information concerned a plot to take over this world by beings who were going to disguise themselves and appear to be from another planet. I know this sounds farfetched, like science fiction or something, but I assure you this is serious. It's going to sound even more outlandish before I finish, so bear with me."

"Is he serious?"

"Has he lost his mind?"

"This is a hoax of some kind."

"Gimme a break!"

The reporters whispered and remained respectful, but it was obvious that they were skeptical.

"These beings are supernatural and they are present on earth right now. We know they are not human because it has been reported that they can walk through walls, change their appearance and size, and even disappear altogether. They possess supernatural strength and, perhaps most frightening of all, they can appear as human beings. They inhabit the earth and take great pains to keep themselves from being identified. UFO sightings and alien abductions are part of their plot to influence the people of the earth and frighten us."

A reporter lifted his hand to ask a question, but the President went on, "The Defense Department had a crew of five people in Germany on a covert mission. This brave crew intercepted messages regarding the conspiracy to take over the world. I regret that they made the ultimate sacrifice for their country and all mankind. The conspirators tracked them down and murdered them. My heart truly goes out to their families. Secretary of Defense Adams was the only one the crew had confided in, and he was abducted by a woman named Lana, the leader of their group."

The President could see some of the reporters shaking their heads and he noticed that they were no longer taking notes.

"Stay with me, now," he implored. "What I am telling you is true. Let me emphasize, these beings are *not human*. They just look human. They have powers that are not of this world and their only mission on earth is to kill, steal, and destroy. I can't explain it all to you in detail, but there is a new book that will explain it. It's entitled *This Means War!* and you will find it in bookstores today. These beings are described and explained in the book."

He went on to explain that copies of the book would be available in most bookstores that day—and assured them that were plenty of copies available to everyone. Millions were being printed!

"I assume that most of you have a Bible in you home. In a way, the Bible is a history book of the evil of these creatures, and the book by the Murphys helps to explain how they operate today in this society. It's important to know that Christians have power and authority over evil, but their power is only activated whenever that Christian believes in it and uses it. I am asking everyone to get a copy of *This Means War!* today and read it for yourself. If you aren't able to get the book, it will be read in its entirety on major TV stations, radio broadcasts, and it will even be on the Internet."

The reporters had resumed taking notes and wondered if they were ever going to be allowed to ask questions. It didn't look very hopeful.

Pausing for a sip of water, the President continued. "We can unite and overcome this threat to our very existence. We must stem the tide of evil before it washes humanity off the face of the earth. We *must unite* and ask God to intervene and bind the forces of Satan and his kingdom, in the Name of Jesus. Thank you, ladies and gentlemen. God bless you—and God bless America!"

With that, the President stepped back and his image disappeared from the screen. The title *THIS MEANS WAR!* appeared in large letters across television screens worldwide and voices began reading the words that Reverend JJ Murphy and his wife had penned. In many languages around the world, the word already was going out.

DELAYED INVASION

18

While someone switched off the television set, Lana stood transfixed, seemingly in total shock and her normally colorless complexion seemed paler than usual. She let out an ear-piercing wail as a look of impending doom filled her eyes. She shook, moaned and swayed back and forth as she wrapped her arms around herself, as if trying to shield herself from danger.

Lana's terror petrified her dependent crew. If Lana fell apart, what hope did they have? She was their leader, their organizer, their guide. Seeing her moan and tremble made them feel insecure and helpless. At the same time, they were rather amused. Could this be the same powerful, confident, malevolent leader they were used to hearing scream foul, vulgar insults at them?

As Lana became more hysterical, she pleaded, "Find a place for me to hide! Please! Please! Our master surely has seen this telecast. I didn't tell him where our new meeting place is, but I know he'll find me. Quickly, you fools! Help me! I MUST HIDE!"

They looked at each other, then stood to their feet, and started toward Lana. They stopped in unison when they felt the air grow cool and foreboding, and a foul stench permeated the room.

Satan stood in their midst! They were filled with dread and panic, prostrating themselves before him.

Immediately worship poured from them! Oh how Satan loved the worship! He preened and grinned, lustful for more adoration, a glutton who never seemed to get enough! He was filled with conceit and contemptuous of those who served him. Even Lana? She looked up at him pitifully.

Yes, even Lana.

Contempt was too much for Lana to bear. She quickly began to flatter in an attempt to appease her master.

"Your plan to invade from outer space was excellent! JJ and Lynn messed it up."

Lana whined, refusing to accept the blame for a plan gone awry. "Please give us one more chance!" she beseeched. "I can get rid of this President and the Murphys. This will all blow over and they will be a laughingstock. You'll still be worshipped by the humans and I will still make an image of you in

God's Holy City. Everyone will worship the image, my lord."

Lana was now crawling toward her master, continuing her desperate appeal. "Please, my master, give us one more chance! We'll come up with some plan to make you the ruler of the world and I promise you we will not fail again. We can get rid of the Christians and everybody, both young and old, will bow down and worship you." Surely that idea would pacify the devil. "That's it, master! We'll get rid of all the Christians, then you will have full reign with no hindrances. It'll be wonderful!"

Lana hesitated a moment, wondering if any of her entreaties were being considered. "Master, I promise we will not fail you again! I promise! This is just a minor setback! Even if the Christians recognize their power, we can deceive them again. They are so easy to deceive!"

Satan's eyes flamed and his nostrils flared! He crossed his arms over his chest and fixed his eyes on Lana, still cowering on the floor. She started to speak again, "Oh, master...!"

"STOP!" Satan bellowed in fury, and the sound reverberated throughout the building. Although small in stature by human standards, he stood erect, like a military officer. He was attractive—after all, he was a fallen angel. But his wickedness knew no bounds.

Lana's tortured pleas had not touched or persuaded her master at all. This plan was dead! And there was nothing Satan hated more than defeat. He hated to lose! And he would not! There must be a way that

Lana could redeem herself. He looked down at Lana giving him worship from the floor.

"You have one year from today."

Then Satan disappeared. But the stench remained.

DELAYED INVASION

19

This Means War! was a success beyond anything the Murphys could have dreamed. Millions of copies were sold by the end of the first day of publication, and a wonderful byproduct was the rapid sale of Bibles around the world. Publishers were struggling to meet the demand for the Word.

All over America, church pews were crowded on Sunday morning. Christians were set free from bondages and hindrances that had held them back from being all that God wanted them to be. Truly *the light* was shining all over the world as never before!

New believers and seasoned believers discovered a new interest in prophecy. There was a new awareness of the exact meaning of spiritual warfare and a desire to learn more. Instead of platitudes, ministers were preaching and teaching truth to their eager flocks. While scholars and saints were confident that they had "dodged the bullet" this time, they wanted to know what was to come and how to prepare for it. The new hunger for truth was glorious!

A mighty worldwide revival was taking place and Christians were becoming united as never before, as they realized that Bible prophecy was being fulfilled. Instead of being crushed by the battle being waged against them, Christians were becoming stronger, more educated in the Word, armed for battle, becoming personally acquainted with the "weapons of their warfare" and it was exciting!

While Christians were sensing victory, Lana was far from conceding defeat. She and her countless subordinates were busy planning new strategy, determined to conquer the "enemy" and ride off in triumph next time. She was thankful that her master had granted her another chance to plan a new line of attack to help him rule and reign on earth! And she could already visualize herself being celebrated as a major player in the victory!

In just a few days JJ and Lynn had made many lasting friends in Washington, D.C. and had entered a world they had never dreamed existed. With the success of the book and the spiritual leadership they afforded renowned government and social leaders, they had been treated like distinguished and illustrious celebrities rather than the humble servants of God they were. They actually had to ask for someone to help them schedule their appointments and handle all the arrangements of meeting people for counseling. How could they refuse to meet with someone the

President requested they see? But there came a point where they had to return to their home. They were exhilarated but exhausted, and the serenity of their home beckoned them. And they knew their beloved cocker spaniel Dudley would welcome them.

Dudley! He had just fathered a litter of puppies right before they left and they were going to keep at least one of them. When they had driven to Washington, they had no idea that it would be anything other then a weekend trip.

Yes, it was time to get home. But this time they didn't drive! Someone had returned their rental car days before and JJ and Lynn were flown home in a private jet.

As they flew, the Murphys sat in comfortable leather seats and smiled at each other.

"Remember how stormy and dark it was when we first drove into town?" asked JJ. It was a rhetorical question, because no one could possibly have forgotten that day. But it was also rather symbolic, because the events of that day had unleashed a very stormy chain of events.

"What a gorgeous contrast!" Lynn replied softly. "Look at that, JJ. Have you ever seen a more beautiful horizon? No storm clouds in that sky!"

Although they had not had an opportunity to discuss it fully because of the crush of activities, they knew they were already very wealthy because of the vast number of books that had been sold. They had hurriedly consulted an attorney and had a contract drawn up, because they were absolute novices in the publishing business. A few days ago they might have considered themselves "greenhorns" but after what they had been through, they didn't feel very "green" in a lot of areas. What a social whirl they had been on!

Well, it was time to slow down for a while, but that could wait until they got home. On the plane they felt happy, carefree, almost giddy, so they gave themselves license to celebrate. Their idea of celebrating? Making a list of ministries they wanted to donate to out of the profits from the sale of the book. They had always wanted to be able to bless others and they resolved to fulfill that dream before they spent anything on themselves. They recognized the Hand of God in all that had happened!

"JJ, we really do need to take a break, you know. We're not getting any younger. In fact, maybe we should retire and enjoy our home and children and grandchildren and Dudley and his new family."

"We'll see, Lynn. We'll see." JJ's reply was pensive and Lynn could see a faraway look in his eyes.

They had called a friend to meet them at the airport and were surprised to see a limousine parked on the tarmac when their plane taxied up and parked.

JJ shook his head. "Look at that! We've come and gone a lot of times out of this airport, but never like this. Can you believe we were just in a private jet? And this limousine. Who ordered this? They must have let Harry know because I don't see him any-where. He'll sure be full of questions when he sees us, won't he?"

Driving into their driveway, JJ and Lynn saw a number of cars parked up and down the street, but paid little attention to them. Little did they know that Harry and a number of their close friends had organized a welcoming party.

They opened the door and heard lots of laughter and noise, but the first "person" they saw was their beloved Dudley, who almost knocked them over!

A big "Welcome Home" banner was strung across the living room and they heard shouts of "We love you—we missed you—welcome back—tell us all about it!"

What a time they had! Their friends grilled them for all the details of their adventure. "What is President Roland really like?" "Did you get to sleep in the White House?" "Did you get to keep the suit, Lynn?" (The answer to that was—yes!) "Do you have any idea where the compound—or bunker—or whatever you call it, is located?" (The answer to that was—no.)

JJ and Lynn almost had to chase everybody out the door because they were getting "mush-brained," as JJ liked to say. Even though they were tired, they were content beyond expression. They had been so honored and thrilled, albeit surprised, to have been greeted by these beloved friends, and their lives were full! True to form, they gave God all the glory for everything.

After saying goodbye to the last guest, Lynn walked up to the bedroom to find JJ sitting at the prized old roll-top desk his father had given him.

"What on earth are you doing, JJ?"

"Don't get upset, Honey, but I feel impressed to write another book. Now that *This Means War!* is a bestseller, I feel I should write another one and let the world know what the Word of God says is going to happen in a short time.

Lynn smiled and sighed, "There goes retirement! Oh well, I would have been bored after a couple of days, anyway, I suppose."

"Do you really feel all right about it? I know you've been through a lot lately and I don't want you to feel under pressure." JJ was a loving, sensitive husband who genuinely valued his wife.

"After a little rest, I'll be ready to go. We need to do whatever we can for the Lord. Anyway, when you really think about, we have all of eternity to take it easy."

Glancing his way, Lynn looked over her shoulder, "I'm beat. I'm going to shower, read the Word of God and turn in." Then, as an after-thought, "By the way, what are you going to name the next book?"

Without even looking up, JJ replied, "*Deceived.* I'm going to tackle the subject as clearly as I can so that millions more can be put on alert and be prepared for Satan's next onslaught. I'm sure he's out there somewhere keeping an eye on Lana and her next strategy. We've all got to be ready!"

JJ continued to write for a short time, then yawned, shut off the computer, and retired for the night.

As JJ and Lynn prayed together they could sense the presence of a multitude of angels surrounding them. If they could have seen into the spiritual realm, they would have seen the huge angels with their swords drawn. These were God's angels on special assignment to protect them, and they were smiling and giving each other a wink of approval as JJ reached for the light.

Warfare Plus Ministries, Inc.

Claire, and her husband Paul, minister nationally and have seen thousands of people freed from demonic influence. They each hold a degree of Ph.D. in Clinical Christian Psychology, and conduct private and group counseling sessions. They also conduct seminars and teach a School of Deliverance.

Other books from Warefare Plus Ministries

THIS MEANS WAR! - A complete guide to the teachings of Christ on deliverance, along with many other biblical references regarding deliverance. Sadly, deliverance has been treated almost like a forbidden topic in the church realm. THIS MEANS WAR! teaches in great depth everything you always wanted to know about demon warfare and the supernatural, but have been afraid to ask!

DEMON SLAYERS - Actual case histories of people who have gone through deliverance. Relive the experiences with them as this book takes you through shocking, extreme, intense battles of Good versus Evil—and Good always prevails!

Warfare Plus Ministries

Product Number	Description	Quantity	Unit Price	Total Cost
BOOKS				
WP-101	This Means War		$12.95	
WP-102	Demon Slayers		$11.95	
WP-103	The Light		$11.95	
WP-104	Delayed Invasion		$11.95	
WP-105	Deceived		$12.95	
AUDIOS				
WP-201	Expose & Expel Demon Power (4 Tapes)		$20.00	
WP-202	Inner Healing/Spiritual D. (4 Tapes)		$20.00	
WP-203	Don't Get Caught In Satan's Web		$10.00	
WP-204	Are You Cursed? (2 Tapes)		$10.00	
WP-205	Power & Authority Over Evil (2 Tapes)		$10.00	
WP-206	If I'm Supposed To Be Gay …(2 Tapes)		$10.00	
VIDEOS				
WP-301	Expose & Expel (4 Videos)		$80.00	
WP-302	Inner Healing/Spiritual D. (4 Videos)		$80.00	
WP-303	Deliverance From Satan's Torment		$20.00	
WORKBOOKS				
WP-401	Expose & Expel Demon Power		$20.00	
WP-402	Inner Healing/Spiritual Deliverance		$20.00	
WP-403	New Beginnings In Jesus Christ		$20.00	
			SUB TOTAL	

Method Of Payment:
- ☐ Visa
- ☐ MasterCard
- ☐ Check

Credit Card Number: _____

Expiration Date: _____

Shipping & Handling
$10.00 & Less	$3.00
$10.01–25.00	$4.00
$25.02–40.00	$5.00
$40.01–60.00	$6.00
$60.01–75.00	$7.00
$75.01 or more	$9.00

USA RATES

Shipping & handling (see chart)

TOTAL

Please Print Clearly

Name _____
Address _____
City _____
State _____
Zip _____

Send To:
Warfare Plus Ministries
4577 Gunn Highway, PMB 206
Tampa, FL 33624

Fax: (813) 908-0228
E-Mail: WarfareP@aol.com